THE NEWLYWED

Gone but not forgotten

THE COLD CASE MYSTERIES #3

ANNA WILLETT

Published by The Book Folks

London, 2023

This book is a work of fiction. Names, characters, businesses, organizations, places and events are either the product of the author's imagination or are used fictitiously. Any resemblance to actual persons, living or dead, events or locales is entirely coincidental. The spelling is British English.

ISBN 978-1-80462-056-4

www.thebookfolks.com

This book is dedicated to my greatest supporters.
You know who you are.

Chapter One

"Why wasn't he at the wedding?" Jane asked. "You've never really explained."

"None of *your* family were there," Richard replied, squeezing her thigh. "We didn't give anyone time to RSVP, remember?"

"I know, but he's your twin. It's different with twins," she said. "They're supposed to be connected at the hip. Besides, it's only a three-hour drive from Seabreak to Perth. Two and a half if you really put your foot down. My parents were in Canada. They couldn't just abandon their cruise. He just didn't want to come. Is that it?"

She was anxious. He could tell by the way she kept turning her wedding ring, twisting it around her finger like it was cutting off the blood supply to her hand. Funny how he could pick up on the little things, even after only a short time. They'd talked about his brother's refusal to attend the ceremony before, but it was obviously still a sore spot. Or maybe she was just nervous. So nervous, it looked like she wanted to rip the ring off her finger. Not that he could blame her. Meeting Edward was big, for *both* of them.

Richard wanted his brother to like her. He wanted her to like his brother, or at least part of him did. Another part of him, the petty part that was still the childish, less attractive twin, wanted Edward to see Jane and be jealous because Richard was the one who'd ended up with a gorgeous wife – not that it would matter to Edward. He wouldn't care what she looked like. But Richard wanted Ed to meet her and see that just like Ed, Jane had that *it* factor. Richard wanted his brother to see that and envy him because he had it all. Because he wasn't a screw-up anymore. Edward would see that if a woman like Jane could love him, Richard had to be a good man. It was a deep need and not one he would ever share. Not even with his wife. But the conversation was now heading into risky territory, and he wanted to get back to feeling smug about how happy they were.

Damn Edward for making him explain on his behalf. How could Richard make Jane understand when he and Edward had never really discussed the situation? If he told his wife he'd begged his brother to come to the wedding, how would that make Edward look? How would that make Jane feel? Why did his twin have to be so blunt, so stubborn? And why, after everything, was Richard still jealous of him?

"It's not like that," Richard replied. "He doesn't leave Seabreak much, it's hard to explain, but he's..." he trailed off, trying to find the right words. After years of training his brain to steer clear of the subject, the words didn't come easily.

He glanced at her and saw her eyes widen and her mouth drop open. Richard had time to wonder why she was so shocked by his response, then there was a *whack*. A sound that reminded him of falling off his skateboard as a kid. The meaty thud and dry dusty crack that followed was almost identical to the sound his knee made when it slapped the pavement. His joint still ached when he climbed too many stairs or jogged for more than a couple of kilometres.

He stomped on the brake as the bird plastered to the windshield slid sidewards and the car fishtailed. The wheel shuddered in his grip and, for one terrifying moment, he was sure the vehicle was about to become airborne. He gritted his teeth, bracing for the inevitable flip. Instead, the tyres squealed, and the car hopped, jerking Richard and Jane forward, then back as they came to a bone-jarring halt.

For a second, they were both silent. Richard staring at the bird, miraculously still glued to the windshield, and Jane breathing in little gasps that sounded like hiccups.

"Oh my God," she managed. "I thought the car was going to flip."

"You and me both," he replied. "Are you okay?"

She nodded. She was unhurt, but her fingers were still clamped on either side of her legs, holding the seat as if she were about to be flung through the windshield. Similarly, Richard was having trouble forcing his hands to release the wheel.

Once his fingers responded, he guided the vehicle onto the shoulder of the road, travelling partially blind because the bird with its wings splayed was stuck on the glass. It seemed impossible that the thing could remain in place after such a dramatic stop. He turned off the engine and let his head rest on the wheel.

"That thing just came out of nowhere," she said in an almost trance-like voice. "I can't believe it flew into the car like that. Do you think it's dead?"

"Looks like it. I'll get rid of it," he said and got out of the car.

It was cool for late February, the sky a marbled grey. He thought about what Jane said about the bird and how it came out of nowhere. Looking at the animal from the outside of the vehicle, with its white and grey feathers and broad wingspan, he could see it was a seagull. Or *used* to be a seagull. The creature's belly was mashed against the glass with blood, thick as oil, coating its legs.

Growing up in a seaside town, he'd seen plenty of dead gulls. Feathered carcasses on the beach or flattened on the roads were not an uncommon sight, but still the idea of touching the dead thing left him cold with disgust. And it *was* disgusting. Dirty feathers paired with the stench of rotten fish spewing out of its spilt guts.

Richard covered his nose with one hand and grabbed the bird's wing tip between his fingers. There was a moment of resistance as it refused to budge, making a wet sucking sound when he pulled. Desperate to be rid of the thing, he tugged harder and the gull came away with a sticky slurp.

"Ugh." He shuddered and flung the creature into the bushes.

When he looked back at the car, he saw a crack in the windshield and Jane's horrified face watching him through a smear of blood and black slimy goo. Her perfect heart-shaped face framed by blood.

He glanced away, not wanting to see the odd look in her eyes. Gazing out to the ocean, where gulls flocked over a passing boat, he sucked in air, trying to clear the stench from his nose. It was odd that one bird would break ranks and fly inland just to fling itself at his car. What was even more odd was standing on the shoulder of the road, trying to fathom the gull's mindless reasoning. Seagulls didn't reason, they scavenged.

Richard wiped his hand on the leg of his jeans and got back in the car. He turned on the windscreen wipers and sprayed soapy water onto the glass, watching the muck spread into greasy-looking smears. After three more sprays, the window cleared, and he started the car.

"That poor bird," Jane said once they were on their way.

"I don't think it would have felt anything. It happened too fast." He glanced her way, still not willing to take his eyes off the road for more than a second. "Are you sure you're okay?" He put a hand on her knee.

"Look, can we stop somewhere?" Jane pushed his hand off her leg. "I need the bathroom and I want to stretch my legs. There's a petrol station coming up. We can pull in there for a while."

"I thought you said you've never been to Seabreak?" he asked.

She turned her head away, looking out the window to where the salt bushes grew in crooked dips, their limbs bent under a lifetime of fierce sea gusts.

"It was a long time ago, when I was a kid," she dropped her voice so he could barely hear her. "I don't even remember the place."

"But you remember the petrol station?" he teased, trying to be playful. Trying to make her forget the near-death experience they'd both just shared with a seagull.

"Jesus, why are you cross-examining me? I don't need you second guessing everything I say," she replied. "I saw the sign, that's all."

The words came with unexpected anger and the *I've just made a joke* grin felt oddly stiff on Richard's face. He wished he could see her expression, because all this was new to him. Knowing Jane was new to him. He wanted to put his hand back on her knee, but couldn't bear another brush off.

"I was just teasing. Look, if it's all too much we can call it off," he offered, half hoping she'd agree and he wouldn't have to deal with whatever was eating at her. And he could avoid seeing Edward because he knew that no matter how charming his wife was, his brother would be unimpressed. The trip had been more Jane's idea than his anyway, but the closer they got to Seabreak, the more agitated she seemed.

"There's no rush, you can meet Ed another time–"

"No." The word crackled like electricity in the air as she swung around to face him. "I mean, we don't have to do that. It means a lot to you and, and–" she seemed to be searching for an explanation "–I'm looking forward to it."

He didn't think she was lying exactly, but looking forward to it? He thought about her wedding ring and the way she turned it like a screw. Looking forward to it felt like a gross exaggeration. Lately, there had been so many times when he thought he had her figured out, but he just kept missing the mark. Still, she was making an effort. The last few months had been crazy for both of them. And that he could count the time he'd known his wife in months was even crazier.

"I know you are," he said. "And a pit stop is a good idea."

Her brown eyes softened, and her lips curved into a smile. One that dimpled her left cheek. He loved that smile. It put him in mind of running his fingers over the small of her back and breathing in the scent of gardenias and jasmine. It reminded him of the way she looked over her shoulder, with tousled blonde hair draped over one eye. It was all still so new; a craving more urgent than love.

Pulling into the petrol station, Richard had the sense that he was re-entering his childhood, only seeing it through eyes that recognised the unadorned scruffiness of a place that had once seemed safe and familiar. Apart from the tailgate of a car parked at the side of the building, the place was deserted. The smiling penguin on the ice chest near the door had faded, the paint chipped away until the bird's face looked ravaged and its expression more of a grimace than a grin.

"I need the restroom," Jane said, heading for the side of the building.

"What do you want to drink?" he called after her, surprised she was in such a hurry.

"Mineral water," she replied without stopping or turning around. "Raspberry."

Raspberry-flavoured mineral water. He watched her, head up, hair bouncing, until she was out of sight. They'd be lucky if the tiny shop had raspberry-flavoured anything. Even plain mineral water was a stretch.

* * *

The ancient coffee machine looked like it hadn't seen a lick of Spray n'Wipe since he moved away seventeen years ago but, after a few seconds of grinding and bubbling, it spurted out liquid that at least smelled like coffee. He filled his cup and then deposited two packets of powdered milk into the drink.

When he was a kid, the place sold everything from Fantales, air-sealed bags of fairy floss to Jaffas – little red balls of orange-flavoured chocolate. Enough sugar to blow a week's pocket money and spend an afternoon dancing in the surf, riding a brain-scrambling sugar high. He thought about buying a bag of Fantales for old times' sake, but the very idea made his fillings ache.

After a few minutes of gazing into the drinks fridge, he settled on a can of lemonade. At least it had bubbles.

When Richard approached the cash register, the girl behind the counter ignored him and continued staring at her phone. He set the drinks down and gave her a few seconds, watching as her blunt thumbs flew over the screen with impressive speed.

The texting, or whatever the hell she was doing, showed no signs of winding up, so he coughed. "Just the drinks, if you have time."

The girl looked up as though unpleasantly surprised to see a customer. Except for pudgy cheeks, her face was flat and there was a large pimple in the crease of her right nostril.

"Yeah, okay." There was impatience in her voice. As she spoke, the pimple seemed to pulse, its anger matching the girl's ill-temper.

Something about the volcanic zit paired with the girl's glowering look got under his skin. He was having a crappy day and no matter how hard he tried – and God was he trying – Jane wasn't happy. To top it all off, the kid behind the counter was treating him like he was a disease.

The girl rang up the drinks with considerably less speed than she'd used on the phone. As Richard swiped his card on the payment terminal, he saw her glance back at her mobile. The petrol station had always been a bit of a dump, but at least the guy who ran it was polite. Well, maybe he was a bit of a tough nut, but he always made eye contact at least. The guy's name was on the tip of Richard's tongue, but he couldn't quite grasp it.

As he put away his wallet, the name came to him. Remembering the car parked at the side of the building, he asked, "Where's Lester? Is he still around?"

"Who?" the girl replied, one hand back on the phone.

"Lester." He suddenly wanted to take the question back and end the interaction so he could get out of the run-down shop and into the fresh air. But he'd set the ball rolling. It would be awkward to just ignore her response. "The man who used to own this place. Do you know if he's still around?"

"I don't know. Maybe." She gave him a disgusted look, irritation cutting her mouth into a lipless line. "Why? You got a problem?"

"I'm just asking a civil question," he said, fed up with her sullenness.

"Look, mister" – she crossed her arms over her breasts – "I just work here."

He thought of telling her that she might as well get used to annoying customers because, with her attitude, she was destined to spend her working life behind one counter or another. The idea of wiping the surliness off her stupid face was almost irresistible but staring into her deadpan eyes, he caught himself and bit back the words. She was just a kid. A bored teenager working a shitty job. In her eyes, he was nothing more than another annoying asshole trying to ruin her day.

"Enjoy the rest of your day," he said with as much sincerity as he could muster.

When he stepped outside, his hands were sweating. He'd almost lost it with a kid and the worst part was, he was pretty sure it had nothing to do with the teenager's crappy attitude. Still unsettled, he looked towards the car, expecting to see Jane waiting, but she was nowhere in sight. He glanced back at the shop, and the penguin on the freezer seemed to smirk at him. The irritation he felt only seconds before morphed into a flicker of anger.

As he stood clutching the drinks, a flock of gulls cawed and circled overhead. A sound that was once so intrenched in his life he'd barely noticed it, now seemed overly loud and invasive. What the hell was he doing? He'd spent half his life desperate to escape Seabreak. To put everything he'd done in the small town behind him. Now he was back with Jane in tow. Why the hell had he let Jane talk him into this trip? He was a man angry with the world because his wife snapped at him *and* he was in the one place he never wanted to see again. Was that love? Because it sure didn't feel like he was floating on a cloud.

He found Jane around the side of the building, sitting at a picnic table. Her back was to him, with her hair floating on the breeze. He felt a familiar stab; longing mixed with anxiety.

Before she heard him approaching, something caught her attention, and she turned her head, startled. The midday sun lit up her hair, creating a halo effect around her profile. A halo of light so clear it felt as if she were beside him. What he saw carved into her features looked like fear. A raw emotion so pure that the gravity of it took his breath away.

The anger he felt only a few seconds ago lost its weight and blew away like a curled-up leaf caught on the sea breeze. She was suffering, and he'd been too consumed by doubts and imagined slights to see it. Or, worse still, maybe he just didn't know her well enough to spot the signs. Perhaps it wasn't fear he'd seen, but something else. Not for the first time, he wondered if she was regretting marrying him.

"You okay, love?" he asked, setting the drinks down.

"Yes," she replied, running a finger under her eye. "Better now."

"This was the best I could do." He sat opposite her and gestured to the lemonade. "The shop's not exactly a gourmet deli."

"It's perfect," Jane said. "Lemonade is my secret vice. A little sugar rush is just what I need." She reached a shaky hand across the table and touched his arm. "And I'm sorry for being such a cow. I'm just jumping at shadows and it's making me, well, a cow. Then that seagull thing." She grimaced.

"Do you ever think you see ghosts?" she asked. "Not actual ghosts," she added before he could answer. "I mean faces from your past? Faces you barely remember that suddenly look so familiar?"

Her fingers were cool on his skin. He wanted to ask why she was so upset because he was sure it was more than just the bird. But things were getting back on track, or at least they seemed to be. Self-preservation kept him from pushing her for more. Or perhaps it was cowardice. Either way, he decided not to rock the boat. Instead of pressing on, asking what she meant by ghosts from the past and having an actual conversation, he told her about the ghost of petrol stations past. He recounted his brush with the disgruntled teenager who served him, hoping the story would make her laugh. When she did, he had the sense it was forced.

Chapter Two

There was a note on the front door. Held in place by a rusty thumbtack, the paper flapped in the breeze.

"Problem with the boat," Richard read aloud. "You know where the key is. Be back tonight. E."

"No dear Richard," Jane said, taking the note out of his hand. "No welcome back." She sounded more upbeat. Even the reproach about Edward's rudeness was light-hearted and tinged with laughter.

"He's a man of few words," Richard replied, setting the suitcase down on the porch.

He wasn't sure why he was defending him. Edward could be an ignorant prick and not because he was thick, far from it. Richard may have got higher marks in school, but Edward was the smarter of the brothers. He was the one the teachers liked. Good at sport, popular without having to try, Edward just didn't care enough to apply himself and somehow, that made him more appealing.

The note, the empty house, it was Ed's way of letting Richard know, he hadn't forgiven him for leaving him to run their father's cray fishing business. It didn't matter that Edward loved the boat and wanted to stay in Seabreak, Richard was the bad guy because he wanted more out of life than running a cray boat. Because he wanted to escape from his past.

The street, always quiet, was almost deserted apart from one car that drove lazily past as he picked up a sun-bleached conch that was imbedded between a Geraldton wax bush and the mailbox. The key was in its usual place, although judging by the number of slaters that curled and scurried when the light hit the dirt, it had been a long time since anyone had used the spare.

"Keeping the boat seaworthy is a full-time job," Richard continued as he walked back along the path that led to the front porch.

"Do you think you should carry me over the threshold?" she asked, crumpling the note. She gave him the first genuine smile he'd seen since they left the city.

He dipped and tossed her over his shoulder caveman style. She gave a cry of surprise and then giggled as he barged through the entrance with one hand clamped on her butt.

"Some things never change," Richard said, setting her down in the main room.

The ocean, immediately visible through the wide expanse of the glass doors, was as much a part of the house as the faded walls. This was his clearest memory of Seabreak. It was an image that came back to him whenever he pictured his home. Not the people or the smattering of businesses, but the constant rolling water. The soughing of the waves, the rushing breakwater and the wind chimes.

"It's beautiful." She said it with oddly begrudging acceptance, the way one might describe a raging fire as having beauty.

Richard couldn't bring himself to answer. Jane was right about the magnificence of the view, but it was also a mournful one. For him, at least. It was a view that reminded him of the vastness and indifference of the world. A place to watch and grieve. A place where he once stood with his father's hand on his shoulder. A reluctant hand that spoke of the man's inability to understand or comfort his son.

"Let's put these bags in the bedroom," he said, leading her away from the glass doors and through the house.

"Which one's yours?" Jane asked, staring at the twin beds.

"The one under the Eminem poster," he said, dumping their bags. "Ed moved into our parents' old room years ago."

"Did you ever sneak girls into your room?" she asked, with a hint of mischief in her voice. "I bet the poster gave you plenty of street cred."

"Help me push these beds together and I'll show you some of my best moves."

When they kissed, her lips tasted like lemonade.

* * *

Jane was unusually quiet as she foraged through the cupboards and fridge. Dusk came with its usual orange splendour, bathing the house in golden light as the wind dropped to a gentle flutter. It had only been a few hours, but Richard was starting to feel like time had moved backwards.

It was a relief to have the house to themselves. It reminded him of the days when he'd beg off school and stay at home with his mother. With Edward at school and his father working on the boat, it was a treat to have her all to himself. While no one ever came out and said it, Mum belonged to Richard while their father and Ed seemed to have their own secret understanding. It was an understanding that suited the family well until his mother died and left Richard as the odd man out. Part of him had never forgiven her for the betrayal.

Her sudden death felt like a deliberately executed exit plan. One that didn't include him. Even now, Richard couldn't think of her without childish resentment tainting his memories.

They dined on scrambled eggs and buttered toast, which they ate seated at the massive dining table watching the sunset. Hungrier than he'd expected to be, Richard devoured his food while Jane picked.

Alone together, he imagined future dinners. Meals that would one day include a child. Their child. After this weekend, he told himself, they'd be happy again. Jane would be bubbly and mischievous, and he'd be less tongue-tied. The problem was Seabreak, not their marriage. Hadn't the disastrous drive into town proved that?

"You grew up here," Jane said, pushing her plate aside. "What was that like?"

She'd been so quiet until now, the question took him by surprise. "I thought we talked about that," he replied. "When we did the whole getting-to-know-you thing."

"Mm." She sounded unconvinced. "You gave me the facts, but that's not the same thing."

He didn't like where this was heading or the way her eyes were trained on his face.

"It was okay," he continued. "Normal stuff. Family, boredom. Small-town life is pretty bland."

"What were the people like? Your friends? Did anything unusual ever happen?"

He set his knife and fork down and wiped his mouth with a napkin. "I had friends – some friends. No one close. I worked on Dad's boat when I was old enough. I hung out on the beach. You know, just kid's stuff."

A look settled on her face that might have been disappointment. He had the feeling he'd let her down somehow or failed a test, so he searched for something to add.

"When I was twenty-one and home from uni, a woman went missing. It was a big deal for a while. Not the usual sort of thing that happened in Seabreak. It kind of divided the town." He shrugged, uncomfortable that he'd shared something he didn't want to talk about. "Something like that changes a place."

"Something like what?" she asked, leaning forward. "What happened to her, do you know?"

Richard got up from the table and gathered up the dishes, glad to have a reason to escape her probing gaze.

"Richard?" she persisted, following him into the kitchen. "What was her name? Was that in 2000?"

"It was fifteen years ago. I don't remember the details." He turned on the tap and dumped the plates in the sink.

"I knew someone who went missing," Jane said.

He flipped a tea towel over his shoulder and turned to look at her. She was back to twisting her wedding ring. No engagement ring because it all happened too fast. *It happened too fast* was something they'd been saying a lot lately. He decided he'd buy her a ring when they got back to the city. Or, he'd ask Ed if he still had their mother's ring.

"She was there one minute and then gone." She let go of the ring and opened the fridge. "No wine."

He was about to say he would go to the bottle shop in the morning when it occurred to him that this was one of the rare times when she'd brought up her past without being prompted.

"Was she a close friend?" he asked.

"No," she said, surveying the meagre items in Ed's fridge. "It was nothing, really. I barely knew her. We should buy wine, don't you think? And salad."

She was wearing an oversized T-shirt and when she leaned into the fridge, one sleeve slipped off her shoulder, revealing the smooth line of her collarbone. The exposed skin gave her a vulnerable look that put Richard in mind of the petrol station. The fear he'd seen when he approached her with the drinks. What could have frightened her like that? He should have asked.

"We should buy a house," she continued. "Near the river. I like the water but not the ocean, it's too relentless.

Something with a nice backyard, not too big, just some grass and a few trees."

It took him a minute to catch up with the sudden change of topic. He couldn't help wondering if she was deliberately trying to change the subject. She was a lot like his mother in that way, always jumping from one thing to the next with lightning speed. There was probably something deeply Freudian about comparing his wife to his mother, but wasn't everyone a product of their childhood? Everything didn't have to mean something.

"A house?" He repeated the words. "What's brought this on?"

"I don't know. Marriage and house, they go together. We can't go on living in your apartment forever. It's too small." She closed the fridge. "It's something to consider. We can go house hunting when we get back."

She walked towards him barefoot and on her toes like a dancer. As she moved, the T-shirt rode up, barely skimming the tops of her long legs. Taking his hand, she pirouetted with surprising grace.

"You, me, room to move." She waggled her eyebrows suggestively. "What do you think?"

He couldn't think because he'd never seen anyone like her. This bed-tousled woman, completely unaware of how spectacular she looked, was asking him to plan a future with her. Just watching her took his breath away. What he felt was no longer craving, but something deeper. Something solid and permanent.

Maybe it had been infatuation when they rushed into marriage. Although he said the words *I love you*, a hundred times, he was never really sure he knew what they meant until he watched the pure abandonment of her moves and his heart broke open. He was in love with her and the knowledge hit him like a warm wave.

Changing the subject or not, her mood had improved, and she sounded excited. That was one of the things that drew him to Jane; her good humour was never far away.

Well, maybe today was an exception, but he hoped not the new rule. Once meeting Edward was over, she'd settle back into her unerring ability to keep things in perspective and laugh at the absurdity of the world.

"I'm tired," Jane said, running her hands through her hair and stretching her arms above her head.

He loved that hair, the way it smelled, the silky feel under his fingers.

"I need an early night."

It was only eight o'clock. Much earlier than their usual bedtime, but it had been a long day. As much as he hoped they'd be together when Edward got home, he couldn't blame her for calling it a night.

"Are you sure you don't want to wait for Ed?" he asked with little hope.

She sighed and kissed him on the cheek. "No, you two catch up and I'll meet him in the morning. I'll be better company when I've had eight hours."

She was heading for the bedroom when he stopped her, pulling her into his arms.

"We're okay, aren't we?" he asked, not caring if he sounded needy.

At thirty-six, he'd never felt this way before. Never so unsure of himself. He'd had relationships that were passionate enough, but none that shook his world. He'd always had the power to stand outside the desire and know what he wanted and how far he was prepared to go. Until he met Jane, and except for a disastrous six-month marriage in his early twenties, the distance was never longer than three months.

Chapter Three

"Moonlight on the ocean."

"Fisherman's devotion," Richard finished, turning to look at his brother.

They were in the main room where Richard was at the table nursing a beer and watching the full moon trail flaxen light over the Indian Ocean.

"You found the place, then?" Edward asked by way of greeting.

It sounded like a joke, but Richard knew it was a jab. Ed's way of admonishing him for not visiting more often. Maybe his way of saying he missed him, but with Ed, you could never be sure.

"I only got lost twice between the petrol station and here," Richard said, watching his brother's back as he headed for the kitchen.

The fridge door rattled as Ed chuckled. He was never one to begrudge a laugh. A moment later, he returned with two beers.

"You started without me," Ed said, seating himself at the head of the table and nodding at the two empties in front of Richard.

"What do you think it means?" Richard asked, ignoring his brother's comment on the empties. "Moonlight on the ocean, Fisherman's devotion."

Ed shrugged. "Who knows? Just something the old man liked to say. Where's the new missus? Don't tell me she's ditched you already."

Richard knew his brother was joking, but the words stung. Less than five minutes together and his twin had homed in on Richard's deepest fear. Or maybe it was just a stupid joke, with no more behind it than brotherly banter. Jab or joke, he could feel heat creeping up his neck and was grateful for the lack of light in the room.

"Jane's asleep. It's been a long day," Richard replied.

"So why the rush to get married?" Ed asked, changing the subject. "You pregnant?"

"Funny," Richard responded with a grin.

"No, seriously, why the rush?" Edward persisted. "After Stella, you always said marriage was for the unimaginative. Did you lose your imagination in that office of yours? I can see how a place like that would suck the life out of you."

Richard was both surprised and irritated that his brother chose now to bring up his ex-wife *and* he remembered Richard's glib remarks on marriage. Remarks meant to be clever and distract their father when he asked why there was no one special in Richard's life. At the time, it was easier to throw out a dismissive line than have an actual conversation with a man who had always been distant and preoccupied. At least, that's how he was with Richard.

Perhaps marriage had changed him because now he wondered if the questions about his lack of interest in settling down had been their father's way of trying to make inroads. In his final year, the old man had tried and Richard had slammed the door in his face. Edward knew it, and so did Richard. Maybe if Richard had met his father halfway, there would be a few decent memories to hold on to.

"People change," Richard said.

"Let's hope so," Ed replied, sipping his beer.

They were silent for a moment. Richard thought of asking his brother what he meant by "let's hope so", but didn't want to risk an argument. Things were awkward enough without Jane waking up to a frosty atmosphere.

"How well do you know her?" Ed asked.

"What are you talking about? She's my wife. I know everything that matters." It seemed like Edward was intent on picking a fight, so Richard didn't try to keep the irritation out of his voice. "Where's this coming from? You think you're Dad now and I'm still…" He shook his head, too angry to finish. Angry over the absurdity of the question and his twin's ability to root out his weaknesses.

Ed simply turned his head and gazed out over the ocean. "If I could, I would have come to the wedding, but you sprung it on me in the middle of cray season. I can't just drop everything and take a few days off, you know that."

It was a lot for Edward. More than Richard's often monosyllabic brother usually had to say on any subject. And possibly as close to an apology as Edward would ever give.

"I know." It was a lame response, but the best Richard could come up with when caught so off guard.

"I don't want to fight," Edward continued. "Believe it or not, I'm happy to see you. If you're happy" – he raised his beer – "I'm happy."

Richard had two choices: continue to be pissed or accept his brother's olive branch. Still rattled by the question of how much he knew about his new bride, Richard raised his bottle and tapped it against his twin's.

"I'm happy," he confirmed.

Chapter Four

Richard woke to the feeling of cold air on his shoulders. Drowsy, he reached for Jane only to find the single bed pulled alongside his was empty. Pulling on a T-shirt, he rolled out of bed. Finding Jane on the back deck, he flopped down on the steps beside her.

"I didn't know you smoked," he said, still sleepy.

"I don't," she replied, blowing out a plume of cigarette smoke. "I used to, but I quit." She turned and gave him a sidelong glance. "Or at least I thought I had. Is this when you say you can't live with a smoker and want a divorce?"

Richard slid his fingers over hers, removed the cigarette, and took a long drag. "We'll both quit tomorrow."

Jane leaned her head on his shoulder and her cheek felt cold against his skin. The smoking thing surprised him, but so what? He'd never told her he used to enjoy a sneaky smoke. What really worried him was finding her sitting alone at almost two o'clock in the morning.

"You have nice shoulders," she whispered. "I don't know how I ever got by without them."

He was about to make a joke about how he'd been working out, but suddenly he thought of his father's attempts at closeness and how he'd shut him out.

Instead of something glib, he said, "You'll never have to get by without them again."

"Then I'll stay right here," she replied, nestling into him.

"What's going on, Jane? If something's bothering you, I wish you'd tell me about it because I'm getting worried – about us." He said the last part around a long breath.

She took the smoke from him and ground it out in the saucer she had in her lap and set it on the step next to a packet of cigarettes.

"It's not us, it's me. I lied when I said I barely remember this place. I remember this place *too* well; it's seared into my brain. The last time I was here, I was fifteen and staying in a holiday house near the caravan park." The words came out in a rush, like a long-held confession.

"I got talking to some other kids who were in Seabreak for the holidays. My parents would have killed me if they knew I was hanging around caravan park people. My mother is such a snob," she said absently.

"One night, I snuck out and went to a party. One of those awful house parties where everyone is stumbling around trying not to look desperate. I got drunk, blind drunk on cheap cider. Everything after that was a bit of a blur, but I ended up alone in the sand dunes vomiting my guts up." She pulled away from him and placed her palm on her forehead.

"I thought I saw something in the dunes, but the next day, I wasn't so sure. I didn't say anything because I was afraid I'd get in trouble. I should have spoken up, but I was a stupid teenager. They'd caught me sneaking out before and my father said if I did it again, he'd send me to boarding school. So, I just pushed it to the back of my mind. Or, at least I tried to."

He felt himself stiffen and forced his mouth to relax before responding. "What did you see?" Richard asked, half afraid he knew what she was going to say.

Jane looked down at her hands. "I think I saw a woman being murdered." She let out a breath. "It's hard to say it out loud."

"Jesus, are you sure?" he prompted. "I mean, did you see their faces?"

"I don't know." Her response sounded agonised. "I've been over it in my mind so many times, I don't know what's real anymore. I don't know what I remember and what my fears have added in. All I know for sure is that coming back here terrified me. And, this is the first time I've ever, well, talked about it really."

The things she was saying, what she was telling him, washed over him like a cold wave. For a few seconds, the pounding of that wave filled his head.

"Okay." Richard couldn't believe what he was hearing. "Slow down and tell me exactly what you think you saw."

"That's just it," Jane replied in a tortured voice. "I don't know. There was a woman, I'm sure of that much. Voices. A man's voice, maybe arguing." She shook her head. "I was lying on the sand, looking up at the stars. I remember my heart was racing, and the sky kept blurring. Maybe I passed out. Then everything happened in flashes.

"I crawled up the dune and saw them. It shocked me because the woman was only half dressed and then I realised the man had his hands around her neck."

The night breeze lifted her hair, and she shivered. "The woman swore, called out something. I think she said *bitch*. That's when I ran. I kept running and stumbling until I fell onto the sand and vomited. I heard someone running behind me. At least I thought I did. I crawled into some salt bushes and curled into a ball." She put her elbows on her knees and dropped her head into her hands. "Jesus, I was terrified. I thought he'd seen me and was coming for me. There were noises. He might have been running, but I couldn't be sure. I'm still not sure of anything."

He couldn't say why, but he had the distinct impression she was holding something back.

"I don't know how long I stayed there, too frightened to move. I barely remember making it back to the house," she finished.

Richard, intent on what Jane was saying, thought he heard something and spun around. Peering through the glass doors behind them, he was sure he saw movement in the main room. Or maybe the sound had come from the dark peaks and hollows of the sand dunes.

"What is it?" Jane asked, grasping his arm.

"Nothing," Richard replied, dropping his voice. "Look, it sounds like you saw a couple having sex in the dunes. Kinky, rough sex maybe, but just sex. It happens all the time – more often than you'd think."

Her face looked bleached of colour in the moonlight. "I don't know, it seemed violent."

"You were blind drunk, you said so yourself. And, just a kid," he insisted. "A kid who saw something shocking and frightening. I'll give you that, but not deadly."

"You really think so?" she asked with a hopefulness that tugged at his heart.

"Yes, I do. Besides," he continued, "if there was a dead woman in the dunes, the whole town would have heard about it. Nothing like that ever happened."

She turned back to the ocean. An ocean that looked black and restless under the moon's glow. "What about that woman you said went missing? It could have been her? Fifteen years ago, would have been when I saw the woman in the dunes."

Richard's breathing felt shallow. "No, that was something completely different. Nothing about what you've said matches up with that incident."

There was a twitch in her jaw muscles. He didn't know how he saw it under the moonlight. If he hadn't been hyperaware of every movement, he would have also missed the narrowing of her eyes. Was it doubt dawning on her face or misery? Why couldn't he tell?

He stood. As eager as he'd been for her to talk to him and share more about her past, this wasn't what he'd hoped for. He wanted the conversation to be over.

"Come on." He offered her a hand. "Come back to bed and stop worrying. There's nothing here to be afraid of."

Jane didn't take his hand. Instead, she picked up the packet of cigarettes from the step and took one out. "You're right and I do feel better, but I'm just going to have one more." She stuck the cigarette in her mouth. "I'll quit again in the morning, promise."

Richard hesitated, not keen to leave her in the dark, pondering what might have been. In the end, he kissed the top of her head. "Are you sure you're okay?"

She tipped her head back to look at him. "I'm sure."

"Don't stay out here too long," he said and went inside.

Later, he wished he'd stayed longer. Wished he'd stayed to see the sun rise with her head on his shoulder and her silky hair touching his chin. But life was just getting good and sleep was still easy.

Chapter Five

"A bit late to be going out, isn't it?" Richard sat at the table yawning and squinting at the morning sun reflecting off the ocean. "It's almost nine o'clock."

He didn't need to elaborate. They both understood that *out* meant on the water. And Edward was wearing a long-sleeved, black rashie. A garment similar to the one their father always wore under his shirt. Only Edward's was made of UPF 50 spandex, nylon instead of the old-fashioned cotton of their father's garb. It was a work uniform of sorts, one Edward only wore going out or coming in from working on the boat.

"Already been," Edward replied, pouring hot water into a couple of mugs. "Had to test the starter motor."

Richard looked around the main room, confused. "So, you met Jane then?"

"No," Edward said, setting the cups down on the table. "She still in bed?"

Richard thought he detected a note of disapproval in his twin's voice. The Wilsons were early risers. *Up before the sun, there's work to be done.* Lying in bed, even while on holiday, was taboo in a fisherman's household.

"She's not in bed," Richard replied. "She was up before me. Wasn't she here when you came in?"

Edward shrugged. "Maybe she went for a walk."

Richard left the table and went out onto the deck. He stood where he'd sat the night before. The saucer was still on the step, stained with ash, but the cigarette butts were gone, scattered on the wind. How long, he wondered, had Jane sat outside in the dark? After scanning the beach in both directions, he returned inside.

"I can't see her," Richard said. "Maybe she went to the shops."

He strode back to the bedroom and found her handbag and phone where she'd left them the night before, on his old desk. Would she go out without her phone? He searched through the bag and found her purse.

Edward had taken up a position over the sink, washing dishes. Richard hesitated for a moment, staring at his brother's indifferent back. When it was clear Edward had nothing to contribute, Richard went to the front door and opened it. The BMW, with its cracked windscreen, was parked in the driveway.

It was baseless, crazy even, but he felt a sinking sensation in the pit of his gut. A sudden drop that left his body feeling heavy with dread. Despite the cool morning air, he had to use his forearm to rub the sweat off his brow to stop it from dripping into his eyes.

Dressed only in a pair of jogging shorts, he closed the door and dashed back to the main room.

"The car's still there," he said to his brother. "Are you sure you didn't see her?"

"Nope," Edward replied, still washing dishes. "I'm beginning to think you made the whole thing up. An imaginary wife, just like your imaginary girlfriend in year seven."

Edward laughed at his own joke and for some reason, the sound of that laughter made Richard want to mash his fist into his brother's face. Before he knew what he was doing, he grabbed his twin's shirt and spun him around.

Clutching the front of Edward's rashie, he pulled him close, within kissing distance and screamed in his face, "What the fuck is that supposed to mean? Why do you always have to be such an asshole?"

Caught off guard, Edward planted both hands on his brother's chest and shoved. The push was hard enough to send Richard stumbling into the stove. Reaching out to steady himself, his hand landed on a hot pan of eggs. He yelped and pulled away, upending the pan and spilling half-cooked eggs onto the floor.

"Take it easy," Edward said, breathing hard. "It was just a joke."

"Do I look like I'm laughing?" Richard replied, cradling his burned fingers.

"Here." Edward ran a tea towel under the tap and offered it to his brother.

Like the unfailing ocean view, Richard realised his relationship with his twin hadn't changed. Within twelve hours, they'd fallen back into their old ways. They could converse one minute and be attacking each other the next, yet somehow, the violent outbursts never lasted. A moment of pure hatred and then normal interaction. He supposed they would look crazy to an outsider, but it had always been this way.

Richard snatched the towel and wrapped it around his hand. "I'm sorry, okay. It's just, well, we talked last night, Jane and I. We had a weird conversation and now she's gone."

"So, you had a fight, and she's gone off to clear her head," Edward offered.

"We didn't have a fight," Richard snapped. "It wasn't like that. It was just, I don't know, strange. She was talking about the past and things that had happened to her." He couldn't bring himself to reveal the details of his wife's story. Not with all the old anger and suspicion it would dredge up.

Edward pulled a wad of paper towel off the roll and bent, scooping runny egg off the floorboards. "Well then, there's nothing to worry about," he said. "She's probably walked to the shops or is sitting somewhere in the dunes."

At the mention of the dunes, Richard darted for the back doors and ran down the stairs. He hit the sand with a thud, still cradling his injured hand. For a moment, he had no idea which way to go, so he just ran.

On the ocean, bright spots of colour darted over the surface of the water as dozens of windsurfers enjoyed the morning breeze. Families were already gathering. Not the masses that congregated on Perth beaches, but a few small clusters of people dotted the sand. No one turned to watch as Richard sped past. Why would they? A shirtless man running on the beach was hardly surprising.

With each thudding stride, his breath burned, and his lungs tightened. He would spot her now, he was sure. She'd appear on the shoreline, long legs dancing just beyond the reach of the rushing tide. Jane would see him running and pick up her pace, a smile lighting her sun-kissed face. Or she'd run out of the surf, hair clinging to her shoulders like damp gold.

But she didn't appear and the further he ran, the more his chest constricted. Veering left, he pounded into the dunes. Gasping as he scaled each mound and half-falling into the hollows. When he finally fell to his knees and looked back, the deck and stairs were out of sight. He'd gone too far, headed in the wrong direction.

The run back took longer and no matter how much he pushed his body, Richard couldn't find his stride. His breathing was short and painful and his upper body bathed in sweat. He jogged three times a week, so why was he struggling? Why was his body fighting against him?

When he reached the house, Edward was waiting on the steps.

"Anything?" he asked.

Richard could taste metal in his mouth and only had the strength to shake his head.

"You don't look good," Edward said. "Just sit for a minute–"

"Can't," Richard replied between gasps, leaning heavily on the rail of the stairs. "Have to go that way." He indicated north.

"You sit here and I'll look," his brother offered.

Richard wanted to refuse. He wanted to keep running because something was wrong. Very wrong. He couldn't say how he knew, yet he felt it with terrifying certainty. With his legs trembling, he flopped onto the step and dropped his head in his hands.

"Okay," he said to his brother, without looking up.

* * *

At noon, Richard couldn't take it any longer.

"We need to call the police," he said. Seeing the look on his brother's face, he added, "I know, but it's the only way."

Edward dropped his head and nodded.

Richard let out a shaky breath. His chest, rather than easing into a normal breathing pattern, had become a solid block of pain.

"I think I might need to go to the hospital," Richard said, clutching his arm.

Chapter Six

Seven years later

"Cases don't get much colder than this," Detective Sergeant Jim Drommel said, addressing the team. "You've had time to review the file, so I'll hand you over to Detective Inspector Pope."

"I'm assuming you've all heard of Richard Wilson," Veronika began. She paused long enough to take in the nods and murmurs of agreement from the three team members seated in front of her. "Bare bones," she continued, "Jane Wilson was first reported as missing by her brother-in-law, Edward Wilson, on February 13th, 2015. Her husband, Richard, suffered a mild heart attack on the same day, so there was some delay between the report being filed and the first time Richard was interviewed. He claimed that the last time he saw his wife was in the early hours of February the 13th at his family home in Seabreak. However, no one saw Jane in Seabreak, and that's where things get cloudy."

Veronika put the file she was holding down on a desk. "What you won't see in the file," she added, "is a proceed with caution warning, but I'm giving it to you now. I know

I don't have to say this, but it bears emphasising. This is a sensitive case, so all enquires are to be framed as simple routine follow-ups."

They were in the briefing room, a lazy rectangle of a room edged with desks – one of the few spaces occupied by SCS, the Special Crime Squad in Perth Central Police Station. Workstations housing computer screens and printers were crammed together, creating a horseshoe of activity. Veronika stood at the head of the room, in front of a collection of whiteboards and an overhead screen. In addition to Veronika and Jim, the team included Detective Senior Constable Stacey Newport, Detective Constable First Class Brian Costa, and the newest addition to the squad, Detective Haru Eccles.

"As you may remember, Jane Wilson's disappearance was a high-profile case. And Richard Wilson hasn't spoken to the police since he sued the department and the lead detective on the case in 2016."

She turned to the board behind her and pointed to one of five images. An A4 size photograph showed a young woman smiling into the camera, her glowing face encircled by a white wedding veil.

"This image ran on every news program and in every publication in Western Australia and became synonymous with the Wilson investigation. But this isn't the woman we're seeking. At least not the image of her the public was fed."

Veronika indicated to the picture above the bridal photo. A less glamorous shot of Jane. Without make-up and careful lighting, she looked younger and somehow more vulnerable. A flesh and blood woman who was more than a glamorous bride. More than a flashy image.

"Jane Wilson, formerly Jane Campion, disappeared on February 13th, 2015, and *she* is the primary focus of this investigation."

Veronika didn't need to explain her decision to focus on the victim and not the prime suspect in her disappearance. Seven years ago, Detective Senior Sergeant David Bender, the lead on the case, focused the entire investigation on Jane's husband. Bender even went as far as declaring Richard Wilson a person of interest during a press conference. Wilson sued the department and won in an expensive defamation lawsuit. The litigation was an embarrassment to the department and essentially made approaching Richard Wilson impossible.

Veronika tapped her knuckles on the image. "This is where we start. Who was she? Who were her friends, her ex-boyfriends, the people who knew her? She worked at Avenue Theatre. Who were her colleagues? We go back over her life, leading up to her disappearance. For every fact that's in the case file, there is always a missing piece of the puzzle. We're starting with bare bones. Let's see if we can put some flesh on them."

She paused for a moment, letting the team absorb her words.

"Jane's parents are aware of what we are doing and will give their full cooperation and support."

Veronika turned back to the photo. "Jane was a knockout, a newlywed who became famous for disappearing, but she was more than a headline and I want to know everything about her before I talk to her husband."

"So, he's agreed to speak to you?" Detective Senior Constable Stacey Newport asked, raising an eyebrow.

"Not yet," Veronika replied. "But I'm working on it."

While Jim gave the three detectives their assignments, Veronika returned to her office and opened the Wilson file. A hard copy file she'd printed out. In some ways, she was old-school, but that didn't make her blind to the outdated blunders that brought the case to a standstill six years ago. And she'd exaggerated when she said she was working on scheduling a meeting with Richard Wilson. In truth, she hadn't made a move on the man.

Approaching Wilson was like stepping onto a minefield. The man was fiercely anti-police, *and* he had deep pockets. Even deeper, since he won his five-hundred-thousand-dollar defamation suit and inherited his missing wife's three-million-dollar estate. The last thing Veronika wanted was another lawsuit against the department.

"Got a minute?" Jim asked from the doorway.

Veronika gestured for him to enter and sit.

"Why now?" he asked. "It's been seven years. Why the renewed interest in the Wilson case? Everyone knows that messing around with Richard Wilson could be a career-ending move, so why is this in your lap?"

"What if he didn't do it?" Veronika replied, sitting back in her chair. "Bender was so certain that Wilson killed his wife, the case was never fully investigated. Not properly."

"Is that why the commissioner okayed it and you agreed to take this on?" Jim asked. "To patch-up Bender's mess?"

"Jane's parents have been pushing for a renewed investigation, so the commissioner signed off on a low-key approach. And I didn't agree," she replied. "I asked for the case."

Seeing the surprise on Jim's face, she continued. "Richard claimed his wife was scared of something. The details are sketchy because by the time he was re-interviewed, it was clear that he was being treated as the prime suspect and he clammed up. And–" Veronika held up a finger while she brought something up on her computer screen "–a woman named Adella Reece went missing in Seabreak in 2000. Fifteen years later, same thing. Maybe there's something in it."

"How did you come across this?" he asked, pointing at the screen.

"I received a missing persons circular about a month ago. The name of the town Seabreak jogged my memory and got me thinking about Jane Wilson," Veronika replied.

"You think someone killed the woman in 2000 and then waited fifteen years and did the same thing again?" Jim sounded sceptical. "Pretty far-fetched theory."

Veronika understood Jim's doubts. She was taking the case in a completely new direction based on nothing but her misgivings about Richard Wilson's guilt, so he was right to question her.

"But not impossible if the two women were linked in some way. Or, if whoever abducted these women has done the same thing in other places. Western Australia is a big place. It wouldn't be the first time someone's travelled the state committing multiple murders and gone unnoticed. Maybe it's nothing" – Veronika shrugged – "but I'm not discounting it – yet."

"So, are we looking for a link or similar cases?" Jim asked.

"For now, I'm interested in finding out what scared Jane Wilson. If we know what she was afraid of, it might point us in the right direction. At the same time, I'm hoping to find something that links Jane to Adella."

"And Bender?" Jim asked. "We'll need to talk to him at some point."

"We'll get to Bender, but first we need to talk to him," Veronika said, spinning the case file in Jim's direction and tapping the page.

Chapter Seven

Caitlin Matthews had embraced the almost decade-long trend in Perth for inner city living. On the ride up in the lift, Stacey noticed an impressive list of amenities available in the building. Gym room, sauna, pool deck and picnic area. Nice digs, but she preferred her late-eighties three-bedroom house. Nothing fancy but a hell of a lot warmer than all the chrome and marble that made up St Andrew's Place. Plus, the idea of sweating away in the gym alongside your neighbours seemed a little too claustrophobic for Stacey's tastes, but each to their own.

When Jane Wilson's one-time roommate opened the door, Stacey realised the woman didn't spend much time in the building's gym room. And, in contrast to the rest of the building, Caitlin's apartment had a stuffy over-furnished feel made even more oppressive by the mingled smells of cat urine and stale cigarette smoke.

"Detective Newport?" Caitlin said, opening the door. "Come through."

"Thank you for agreeing to talk to me," Stacey said, following the woman through to what would have been a spacious living area if not for the stacks of papers and cardboard boxes.

"Sorry about the mess." Caitlin twirled her fingers in the air. "But I work from home, so it gets a bit cluttered."

"I understand," Stacey said, picking her way around a side table stacked with dusty bubble wrap.

"I was a bit surprised to hear from you," Caitlin said, settling herself on a sofa next to an overweight, sleeping ginger cat. The animal was so still, Stacey wondered if it was real or stuffed.

"I haven't heard from the police in six years." She tapped a finger to her chin. "No, it's closer to seven years." She gestured for Stacey to sit.

Wearing a brightly coloured kaftan that did little to hide her obvious bulk, Stacey couldn't imagine the stunning blonde in the case file photos having much in common with this somewhat dishevelled woman. But, then again, people change. She might not be a knockout like Jane, but Caitlin had the good fortune to age and go on with her life. Jane wasn't so lucky.

"As I mentioned on the phone, this is just a routine follow-up," Stacey said, sitting on the edge of an armchair dusted with a generous coating of cat fur.

"Hm." Caitlin bunched her lips into a disappointed pout. "I thought you might have been coming to tell me you'd found her. But I suppose that wouldn't make much sense, because why would you be notifying me and not her parents? I'm sure they would have let me know."

"Or husband," Stacey added.

"Oh yes," she replied. "But I sort of thought he'd be out of the loop."

Stacey waited, giving the woman time to elaborate.

"I don't know how these things work, but with him being the one that you think hurt Jane, it would make sense that you'd contact her parents first," Caitlin continued. "But you haven't found her, have you?"

"No," Stacey replied, "but I do have a few questions, if you wouldn't mind?"

When Caitlin nodded for her to continue, Stacey took out her notebook. "When was the last time you saw Jane?"

"That would have been just before she went missing. She came around to the flat to pick up some things." Caitlin smiled. "She was looking for her red bikini. She still had most of her things at the flat so she often popped over."

Stacey thought for a moment. "But she'd been married for two months. Why hadn't she taken her things?"

Caitlin reached out and stroked the ginger cat at her side. To Stacey's relief, the animal proved he was alive by stretching his front paws.

"I'd wondered about that," Caitlin replied. "But Jane said Richard's place was too small. I did not know she owned the flat we'd been sharing until *after* she disappeared."

"A funny thing to keep secret," Stacey offered, hoping to draw the woman out. "Why do you think she kept that from you?"

"Jane was a very private person. Don't get me wrong, she was lots of fun and sort of compelling." Caitlin looked off towards the window where the view took in the distant hills. "She had this way of making you feel special, like you were really seen. Jane was a good listener. But she wasn't one to prattle on about herself."

Stacey thought she saw tears in Caitlin's eyes and couldn't help wondering if the woman's feeling for her long-lost roommate went deeper than friendship.

"How did she seem?" Stacey asked. "That last day when she dropped by?"

Caitlin appeared confused for a second, lost in her memories. "She was her usual self, jolly and playful."

"Was she worried about anything?" Stacey probed.

"No." Something about the way the woman drew out the word made Stacey think she had more to say.

"Just," Caitlin continued, "when she mentioned where they were going, Seabreak, Jane seemed, I don't know, sort of resigned."

"How so?" Stacey asked.

"She said the name of the place like she was dreading it. I put it down to the whole meeting the in-laws thing."

Stacey nodded and made a note. "What about ex-boyfriends? Was there anyone else in the picture that might have been causing Jane problems?"

"There was someone, but Jane ended it when she met Richard." Caitlin frowned. "I told the police all this, years ago, and the detective wrote it down, just like you're doing now. I'm sure if it was important, he would have looked into it."

Stacey had read the Wilson file thoroughly. She had even committed the most salient sections to memory, but she couldn't recall any mention of an ex-boyfriend. She wasn't surprised that Detective Bender had left the information out of his case notes. At the time, he, like everyone else, had Richard Wilson pegged as a murderer. Even now, Stacey wasn't convinced otherwise. Still, it was negligent and highly unprofessional of Bender to manipulate the file so everything pointed in one direction.

"Do you remember the ex-boyfriend's name?" Stacey asked.

Caitlin continued to pat the cat, not meeting Stacey's eyes. She had the distinct impression the woman was playing for time. "No," she finally answered. "I don't remember Jane telling me his name. Why? Do you think he was involved?"

"As I said," Stacey answered, "this is a routine follow-up, so it is necessary to go over old ground. To check facts and jog memories." The explanation didn't sound terribly convincing, but Caitlin was nodding. "Just recount as much as you can remember."

Twenty minutes later, Stacey was on her way out of the apartment when she remembered something Caitlin mentioned earlier.

"You said Jane kept some of her belongings at your old flat. What happened to her things?" Stacey asked.

Caitlin paused, one hand on the door. "I thought Richard would have got in touch, but I never heard from him." As she spoke, the ginger cat appeared between her legs. "In the end, I telephoned Jane's mum, and she sent Jane's dad to pack them up. I don't know if she kept them or donated everything. I did ask her about Richard though."

"What did she say?" Stacey asked, sure she already knew the answer.

"She said that he'd murdered her daughter, and she'd make sure he paid for it."

Chapter Eight

Jane Campion's parents were older than Brian had expected. He wasn't sure why he'd expected a younger couple, maybe because the missing woman he'd seen in the photographs looked so young and vibrant. It made it hard to believe she'd sprung from two such frail people. But he knew grief could suck the life out of even the most robust person.

He also remembered seeing Marian and Stephen Campion on a news conference appealing for information during the first desperate weeks of the investigation. Once he received the Wilson file, Brian had found the clip online and watched it with renewed interest. When he viewed the footage, he noted two things; Jane's father appeared crushed. A man moving with the sluggish gait of someone heavily medicated. And the glint of anger in his wife's eyes.

The glint was still in Marian's eyes, no longer burning with such ferocity, but the embers remained. Despite her now trembling hands, Brian didn't think it would take much to reignite the fire.

"I'm grateful that you're putting a renewed effort into finding my daughter, Detective, um?"

"Costa," Brian responded. He indicated to Haru, who was seated on his left. "And this is Detective Eccles."

They were on the Campion's stylish but dated alfresco area. Over the woman's shoulder, Brian could see the green-blue waters of the Swan River.

"Do you have children, Detective Costa?" Marian Campion asked.

Brian glanced at his partner, thrown off stride by the woman's question.

Deciding there was nothing to be gained by being evasive, Brian answered. "Yes, two."

"Well," she replied. "It's been seven years and six days since I last saw my child, so you'll understand I'm eager to get things moving."

He'd been mistaken about Marian. He now realised it wasn't fire he'd seen in the woman's eyes, but ice. Cold, hard and frozen. Or maybe time had turned the fire to ice.

"Of course." He'd been about to ask the woman when she had last seen or spoken to her daughter, but she'd already made that date abundantly clear. "When you saw Jane, how did she seem? Was she nervous? Worried about anything?"

"If by worried you mean, did she seem like a woman who thought her husband was planning to kill her, then the answer is no. If she had," Mrs Campion continued, "do you think I would have let her go?" Her voice cracked on the last two words.

Despite the woman's hard exterior, he could see she was still suffering. He thought of his own kids and couldn't begin to fathom what the couple must have been going through. He only wished he knew what, if anything, he could say to offer her some comfort, but only promises would do. And anything he promised would be a cruel lie.

Brian tried to make his next words as gentle as possible. "So, she seemed happy? Looking forward to visiting her husband's brother in Seabreak?"

Mrs Campion closed her eyes. "I've gone over that last day a million times and all I can say is Jane gave no indication that anything was amiss. Yet she was worried. I always knew when Jane was worried. Scared even."

Brian's phone vibrated in his pocket but he left it and continued to focus his attention on the Campions. He had one chance to win them over. To make them understand that the police were committed to finding Jane and not just going through the motions.

"Jane was nervous," Mrs Campion continued. "She wanted the meeting to go well, but…" she hesitated. "My daughter wasn't fond of Seabreak. I don't think she relished the idea of returning there."

"She'd been there before?" Brian asked, surprised by this new piece of information.

"Oh yes, when she was fifteen, we took a holiday in the town. I remember Jane didn't enjoy it. In fact, she said on more than one occasion that she'd never return." Marian looked at her husband for confirmation.

"She was a sensitive girl." It was the first time Stephen had spoken and his voice sounded rusty, like an old gate in need of oil. "After that trip, she became quite withdrawn."

"Yes, well, teenage girls can be emotional, sullen even," Marian jumped in. "There was a party which we wouldn't allow her to attend. It led to a bit of teenage angst, nothing more."

Something in the way Stephen Campion used the word *sensitive*, together with his wife's rush to brush off his observations, set off alarm bells. Brian was sure there was more to Jane's aversion to Seabreak than her mother was letting on. Whether that aversion or Jane's *sensitivity* had anything to do with her disappearance fifteen years later, he wasn't sure, but it was worth pushing for more.

Brian turned his attention to Stephen. "You said Jane was a sensitive girl, withdrawn. How so?"

"It was nothing really." Marian answered for her husband. "She attended a few counselling sessions, and that was it. Not uncommon in girls of that age."

It was a touchy subject, so Brian decided to let it go for now.

"What do you think happened to Jane?" he asked, looking first at Stephen and then at Marian.

Before Stephen could speak, Marian took the lead. "I think her husband murdered her." She hit the word *husband* with bitter sarcasm. "I don't think our daughter ever made it back to Seabreak. I think, no, I know the police bungled this case the first time, and Richard got away with murder."

A few awkward moments later, Marian offered to show Brian and Haru to the door. Before standing, Brian took out his phone and read the text message he'd received from Stacey.

"One last thing, Mrs Campion," Brian said. "Jane's friend, Caitlin, mentioned you collected some of your daughter's things from her old flat. Would it be possible to have a look through those items?"

Marian raised her brows in a tired gesture. "You may as well. I'll give you the address and key to our storage unit. Everything belonging to our daughter is in there – we've kept all her things just in case..."

Chapter Nine

"Did you ever consider country policing?" Veronika asked.

"I don't know if Mandurah counts as a country post anymore," Jim replied. "Don't tell me you're thinking of making a move?"

"No," she answered quickly. "I don't know, just thinking about the future."

After last night when her son, Tony, announced his plans to move in with his girlfriend, Veronika's mind was only half on the case. It shouldn't have come as a surprise; Tony was an adult. At age twenty-two, it was only natural he'd want to spread his wings and go out on his own. Verity was a nice girl, she made Tony happy. What more could Veronika ask for? So why had the announcement hit her so hard?

They were on the Forrest Highway, approaching the food and petrol hub. The endless vista of farms and bushland gave the feeling of being in the countryside, although they were less than an hour from the city.

"You want a coffee?" he asked, pulling onto the roundabout.

"I'll have tea," Veronika said, leaning back and stretching her legs. "I'm cutting back on caffeine."

Ten minutes later, they pulled out of the petrol and food hub. Ten minutes after that, they were heading towards Mandurah Police Station.

"You know we could have done this by phone," Jim said, sipping his coffee. "It would have been a lot quicker."

"Maybe," Veronika replied. "But I've never met Sergeant Culla, so I need the face-to-face time. He was the first officer to take Richard Wilson's statement and I have to make sure of what I'm getting and that he's doing more than regurgitating his old notes. I can't do that unless I'm sitting across from him."

"I thought someone with your years in the job knew everyone," Jim said with a sidewards glance.

Veronika couldn't help but laugh. "My years in the job? I'm not a dinosaur yet."

Over the years, they'd fallen into a comfortable working relationship. More than that, Veronika considered Jim Drommel to be a friend. She may have outranked him, but he'd always been there when she needed him. He'd even saved her life a few years back. Of everyone she worked with, Jim was by far her most trusted partner.

"Besides," Veronika continued, "he might have been involved in the Adella Reece investigation in 2000."

"You still think there's a connection between Adella and Jane's disappearance?" he asked.

Before she could answer, her phone beeped. It was Brian. He gave Veronika a brief rundown on his interview with the Campions.

"Do you want us to go ahead and search the storage unit where Jane's things are kept?" Brian asked.

Veronika gave him the go-ahead, reminding him to get Jane's parents' permission to remove any items that might be worth looking at.

"And, Brian," she said before hanging up, "let me know if you find anything important."

When she tucked her phone away, Veronika stared at the windscreen, no longer noticing as the scenery changed from farms to buildings.

"What?" Jim asked.

"It seems Jane visited Seabreak fifteen years before she went missing. Around the time Adella disappeared," Veronika replied.

"Coincidence?" Jim suggested half-heartedly.

She took a sip of her tea before answering. She experienced a ticking sensation as her heart worked to keep pace with her mind. It was a familiar feeling, one of forward momentum. A sense of facts coming together.

"I don't believe in those," she replied.

* * *

Bob Culla's career trajectory wasn't unusual in the force. There were plenty of officers whose professional lives plateaued. Good solid men and women who were content to see out their working years on the force without striving for advancement.

When Culla greeted them and showed them to his office, Veronika *was* surprised by how trim and efficient the man appeared. She was also struck by his full head of hair; blonde and thick, greying only at the temples. She'd had him pegged as an ageing portly man, biding his time until retirement. Seeing how off the mark she was, Veronika chided herself for her preconceived notions. Yet at the same time, she couldn't help but wonder how such a man could be content to see out his career as a sergeant in various country postings.

"I dug out my old notebook," Culla said, laying his hand on the dog-eared book on the table in front of him. "The Wilson case was the biggest of my career. I've gone over it in my mind so many times, it's carved into my memory."

"I know what you mean," Veronika replied. "Some of them stick with you, even the closed ones."

Unbidden, she had a sudden memory of her last big case. Not of the man she finally arrested, but of a woman she interviewed. The girlfriend of one of the victims. Even after more than thirty years, her sorrow was still fresh, almost palpable. It was the ones who were left behind that carved themselves into Veronika's memory. But, right now, the image of Jane Wilson, looking fresh-faced and hopeful, was at the forefront of her thoughts.

"Tell us about your initial meeting with Richard Wilson," Veronika asked. "I've read your report, but if you wouldn't mind, I'd like to hear it from you."

Culla's office was roomy by police standards. Enough space for the three officers to fit comfortably around his desk. On the right, a window looked out over a patch of manicured lawn rimmed with trees. In the distance a glimpse of ocean sparkled.

"So, you *are* reopening the case?" Culla asked.

"That's still to be determined," she responded.

With such a high-stakes inquiry, it was prudent to keep as much information as possible strictly within the Special Crime Squad.

Culla looked sceptical, but nodded his agreement.

"If you read the file," he began, "then you know the first person I spoke to was Edward Wilson. I met him at Seabreak Infirmary. He didn't give me much detail, just that his sister-in-law was missing. He didn't seem particularly worried about her, which was understandable at the time."

"How so?" Veronika asked.

"Well, his brother was being treated for what they thought at the time was a heart attack. Edward was distracted, more concerned with his brother. Jane had only been unaccounted for a little over twelve hours."

"Wait a minute," Veronika broke in. "What they thought at the time was a heart attack? The file notes say that Richard had a mild heart attack."

Culla gave a wry smile. "A few hours after first meeting him, Edward Wilson described the incident to me as a heart scare. Later, the brothers claimed I'd misunderstood, and Richard had indeed suffered a mild heart attack. As you know, without a warrant, I didn't have access to Richard's medical records. I had no way of confirming what exactly Richard was treated for."

Veronika didn't bother asking Culla why he'd never tried to get a warrant. They both knew that, under the circumstances, there was no good reason for a warrant to be granted.

"So, Edward filed the initial report?" Veronika prompted. "But he seemed unconcerned about his missing sister-in-law?"

"Like I said," Culla continued, "it hadn't been twenty-four hours since Jane was last seen. Back then, I half-believed, no, ninety per cent believed, that the whole thing was newlywed drama. Based on Edward's attitude, I think he felt the same way."

"Did you think the heart attack thing was Richard's way of buying time?" Jim asked.

Culla turned his attention in Jim's direction. "Not at the time."

His response was clipped, almost defensive. Veronika could only imagine how many times Bob Culla had been asked to explain why he hadn't acted on Jane's disappearance sooner.

"I thought the poor bloke was just in a state because of the wife's absence," he continued. "You know, just married and the new missus ups and leaves."

"So, it was another day before you spoke to Richard?" Veronika asked, trying to move the story along.

"Yes," Culla replied, opening his notebook and glancing down. "I visited the Wilson brothers at their house in Seabreak. By then, no one had seen or heard from Jane for thirty-six hours. Before I arrived at the house, I contacted Jane's parents, hoping she'd been in touch. Judging by their reaction, I realised it was out of character for their daughter to drop out of contact, and I became concerned." He held up a hand. "It was mild concern, but I *was* getting a bad feeling."

He didn't need to elaborate. Both Veronika and Jim knew the feeling he was describing and how quickly a run-of-the-mill inquiry could turn into something grave.

"When I arrived at the house," Culla continued, "I saw a BMW parked out front next to Edward's ute. It was only when I passed the car that I noticed the cracked windscreen. I remember stopping to take a closer look and that's when I saw what appeared to be blood."

Veronika remembered this section from Culla's report. So far, he'd described the moment almost word for word. This was a practised response.

Wanting more than she could read in the file, Veronika pushed. "What were your thoughts?"

Culla scratched his head. "Alarm bells. Richard obviously hit something. Something that bled."

Something that bled. The words carried their own weight.

"And what was your initial impression of Richard Wilson?" she asked.

He held her gaze for a moment before answering. "My impression. Does it matter?"

"I believe so," she responded.

"I know he seemed pretty robotic going in and out of court, but that day, when I spoke to him, he looked rough. Sick, exhausted and frightened. The first words out of his mouth were, *have you found her?* Maybe he's a good actor or I'm not as sharp as I thought I was, but he seemed genuine. But," he added, "Wilson was a smart guy. What better way to avoid questioning and play the devastated husband than by faking a heart attack?"

"But no one could corroborate his version of events," Veronika concluded.

"No," Culla said around a tight breath. "No one saw Jane Wilson in Seabreak. The girl at the petrol station confirmed that Wilson stopped there and bought two drinks. But she never saw the wife."

They were silent for a minute, absorbing the facts. Most of the case against Richard Wilson, although scant, was predicated on the belief that Jane never made it to Seabreak and so everything Richard reported was a lie.

"Sergeant Culla," Veronika began, "what can you tell me about Adella Reece?"

For the first time since the meeting began, Culla seemed thrown. "I haven't heard that name in a long time. Why do you ask?"

"As I said," Veronika replied, "all matters are still to be determined."

There was a slight tightening around Culla's mouth and he glanced from Veronika to Jim. Obviously, he wasn't used to being the one answering questions.

"She went missing in 2000," he responded. "I hadn't been in Seabreak long. I was still a constable, so I wasn't involved directly in the investigation."

"Mrs Reece was never found, correct?" Veronika asked. "Do you recall the general assumptions made by your colleagues concerning Adella's disappearance? Suspects? Potential scenarios?"

Culla pushed out his bottom lip and glanced at Jim for a second time. "She had a lot of friends. Male friends, if you know what I mean."

"She was the town bike?" Jim offered in a matter-of-fact way.

It was a comment that was completely out of character for Jim, but no matter how jarring she found the characterisation of the missing woman, Veronika kept her expression neutral. Jim was speaking a language that a man like Culla, who came up through the ranks at a very different time, would understand. Jim was essentially putting the sergeant at ease and giving him a green light to speak freely.

Culla raised his eyebrows. "There were some who said that. You know what they say about small towns and small minds. In my experience, it's often true."

The man's pragmatic response surprised Veronika. Bob Culla might be a small-town cop, but he was adept at ducking and weaving.

"Mrs Reece struggled with depression and alcoholism," Culla went on. "The general consensus was suicide. Her bag and shoes were found on the beach. She wouldn't have been the first person to decide to walk into the ocean."

"When Jane went missing," Veronika said, "did you consider the possibility of a link between Adella Reece's disappearance and Jane's? Seabreak is a small place. I'm guessing women don't just vanish there every day."

Culla's features stiffened for a second and then relaxed. He appeared to be exasperated and trying not to show it.

"There was no link. Two very different circumstances fifteen years apart." He spoke slowly and deliberately. "If there was anything, and I mean anything linking the two women, I would have flagged it."

Chapter Ten

"It's been a while since anyone's been in there," the manager of the storage facility said, leading them along lines of shuttered units. "You guys working on that Wilson woman's disappearance or something?" he asked, stopping and gesturing towards an anonymous-looking shutter.

"Something like that," Brian responded. When the manager, a skinny man with a tuft of unruly white hair, remained beside him, Brian added, "We'll take it from here."

The storage locker, one amongst hundreds in a sprawling, single-storey concrete structure on the outskirts of Subiaco, was larger than Brian expected. When Haru unlocked the roller door, it took both men's strength to push the shutter up high enough for them to enter. Obviously, while Marian Campion felt the need to keep her daughter's belongings, that need didn't extend to visiting the collection. But, why would it? Brian could imagine handling the long-forgotten items would only drag the grieving mother deeper into sorrow.

"Is that a car?" Haru asked when the overhead lights stuttered to life.

"Jesus," Brian responded, taking in the enormity of the items. He nodded to the shrouded hulk that was clearly a small vehicle. "They really *did* keep everything. I can't believe there's nothing in the case file about this place. Detective Bender notes visiting Jane's old flat, going through her things and finding nothing of interest, but who knows what that meant."

There were rails of clothes draped with clear plastic, archive boxes stacked in piles as well as furniture and books. This was Jane Wilson's life, an assortment of outdated clothes and furniture contained within the bare concrete walls.

"How do you want to do this?" Haru asked.

Haru had been with the squad for over a year. In the beginning, Brian wasn't sure if the detective constable had what it took to work on cold cases. Most young officers were hungry for action, not the often slow plod of going over old ground that was involved in historical crimes. Haru, however, had surprised Brian with his calm, methodical approach.

"We start with the boxes," Brian replied. "Photograph and list anything we take. We're looking for journals, diaries, letters, photographs, receipts. Anything that could give us a picture of her life leading up to her last days."

The cartons contained everything from old make-up to netball medals. The items were boxed haphazardly, suggesting someone had hurriedly emptied draws and cupboards. Jane's father had done the job. A rushed job, working fast, not wanting to pause and linger over his daughter's belongings or what packing them away actually meant.

"I've got some photos," Haru said, holding up a large envelope.

Most of the images were of Jane and other young women. There were a few pictures of what looked like a mountain range and a river, and some older images of a small brown dog. Flicking through the collection, Brian paused on a photo of Jane, clearly recognisable as a teenager sitting on a log fence with the ocean behind her. He turned the picture over. One word; Seabreak. Shuffling back through the collection, he noted that this was the only snap that someone had bothered to write on.

"No family photos," Haru pointed out.

"Her father would have taken those," Brian said, still looking at the Seabreak picture. "Bag these up and put them on the list."

An hour into the search, Haru helped Brian pull the tarp off the car once driven by Jane Wilson. When the heavy cover lifted, he got a whiff of damp air and a face full of dust.

The paint work on the silver Mazda 3 looked dazzling under the overhead lights. Jane's parents hadn't thought to give them keys for the vehicle, so when Brian tried the driver's door, he was relieved to find it unlocked. Rather than going straight to the glovebox, he slid behind the wheel. Even though the interior of the car looked to be in almost pristine condition, the air inside had a stagnant smell. Maybe it was his imagination, but he thought he caught a hint of perfume. Something floral; the scent of gardenias so faint it was nothing more than a ghost.

Turning his attention back to the car, he reached over and opened the glovebox. Sunglasses, an open packet of cigarettes, a small box of tissues and a stack of papers. On closer inspection, he saw the slips were in fact machine-generated parking dockets, all purchased at the same facility. Something or nothing? Each ticket had a timestamp. The same time and day, a Tuesday, but all two weeks apart and dated between June 2014 and January 2015.

Brian pulled a Ziploc bag out of his jacket pocket and dropped the slips of paper inside. Next, he searched the console where he found a few CDs, a couple of dollars in change, and a pale green scarf. There was the scent again, stronger as he lifted the scarf. On impulse, he bagged the silky fabric and stuffed one of the CDs into his pocket.

"Got something." Haru's appearance at the open car door startled Brian.

"It was in one of the books." He held a dog-eared paperback in his hand. "I only found it when I lifted a stack and this one fell on the floor."

Brian stepped out of the car and took the book. Holding it open to the page Haru showed him, Brian saw a newspaper clipping. A yellowed rectangle of print with a two-paragraph report and a headline.

Local Woman Missing

Assuming the report was about Jane Wilson and perhaps placed in the book by one of her parents, he scanned the text. There was no date and, after reading the details, he quickly realised that it wasn't about Jane Wilson, but another woman. A woman the report identified as Adella Reece.

"There's something in the margin," Brian said.

A word penned in blue ink? Age had dulled the scrawl to little more than a smudge, but a *D* was clearly discernible. He wondered if the smudge was once a name.

"So why did she keep a clipping about a missing woman? Maybe she was a friend?" Haru asked.

"Strange," Brian replied. "But it was important enough for her not only to keep, but to hide. Bag it with the rest of the stuff."

After twenty minutes spent leafing through Jane's extensive collection of paperbacks and finding nothing but a few old bookmarks, Brian left Haru to continue and he moved on.

Before leaving the storage unit, Brian pulled the plastic off one of the racks and stared at the clothing. Expensive garments in bright colours and made of what looked like rich fabrics. Jane Wilson was a woman who enjoyed beautiful things. Something of that woman was still very much alive in the concrete room. And, at the same time, she was painfully absent.

What was it about this place, Brian wondered, that had his mind working in an almost poetic way? The idea made him cringe. He was a rational man. He worked on facts and supporting evidence, so why was he romanticising the missing woman's belongings?

"That's about it," Haru said, holding a box of items.

"Yeah," Brian answered, and dumped the scarf in the box. "That's it."

A moment later, Haru shut off the lights and the concrete room returned to darkness.

* * *

After leaving the office for the day, Brian put the CD on in his car and listened as the music began. He didn't recognise the name of the singer, Nina Simone, but her voice had a rich deep quality. He wasn't given to emotional responses, yet her words and the tone of the song put him in mind of loneliness and a world of experienced sorrow. The idea of Jane Wilson in her modern car wearing bright colourful clothes seemed at odds with the gravity of this songstress. What he felt was outside the scope of his training as a cop, yet he was certain that Jane was suffering under the burden of something significant.

Chapter Eleven

When Veronika arrived home, her mother was folding laundry while calling out answers to a quiz show on the TV.

"I can do that, Mum," Veronika said, gesturing at the basket of towels.

Mary-Lynn waved a dismissive hand. "It's nothing. If you want to help, start washing the lettuce and chopping the capsicum."

This was a familiar routine. Since the birth of her son twenty-two years ago, Veronika had lived with her mother, sharing the burden of raising Tony and establishing a home. As a single mother and a newly graduated police officer, the demands of shift work made taking care of a young child a two-person job. Mary-Lynn had willingly spent her retirement years filling the second half of that job, a commitment that Veronika was eternally grateful for.

Before starting on dinner, Veronika dumped her bag and laptop on the coffee table. "Just the two of us," her mother said, pre-empting her daughter's inevitable question. "Tony's dropping some of his things off at

Verity's flat and she's making them curry or satay, I'm not sure which."

"So, he's definitely going ahead with it?" Veronika replied.

Mary-Lynn pushed her glasses up, setting them to rest on her grey hair. "Yes, darling, he's going ahead with the move. Of course, he is."

Veronika recognised her mother's tone. The one she used when Veronika was a child and grappling with unwanted truths. A fatalistic yet gentle way of explaining those hard truths.

Veronika nodded. "I'll start on the salad."

They ate with plates on their laps, watching the news.

"He's not home much anymore, so it won't be so different in that way," Veronika said, pushing a piece of cucumber around her plate.

"You'll probably see more of him, if anything," Mary-Lynn replied. "He'll be visiting, so when he *is* here, it will be because he wants to spend time with you. For the past few years, he's been more of a ship passing in the night."

She knew her mother was trying to make her feel better, and everything she was saying made sense. Yet Veronika couldn't escape the feeling that a part of her life and maybe identity was ending. Was she ready for that change? Probably not, but she supposed she'd have to get ready or risk becoming a tragic cliché. An empty nester: even the words made her cringe.

She told herself that Tony wasn't disappearing from her life, but in some ways, it seemed like she could already feel his absence. What, she wondered, did it feel like for Jane Wilson's parents? And for Richard Wilson? If he was innocent, how intolerable would that loss be when compounded by the pain of knowing the world had branded him as a killer? These were questions she asked herself because they were germane to the case, but also to distract herself from thinking about how *her* life was about to change.

"I have some files to go over," Veronika said, taking the dinner plates through to the kitchen. "I'll put these in the dishwasher."

Upstairs in her bedroom, it was Adella Reece's file she pulled out of her bag. Compared to Jane's case file, it was sadly thin. A few witness statements, a couple of police reports, and a photograph.

Two women, Adella and Jane, missing from the same small town fifteen years apart. Not enough to ring alarm bells. Not yet. What troubled her was the intersection of Jane and Adella's lives. Two missing women who had, at one time, been in the same place, at the same time that one of them disappeared. Veronika's gut told her it meant something, but what?

She made a note to have someone on the team run a check on missing women between Jurien Bay and Two Rocks in the last twenty years. If Jane and Adella crossed paths with each other, maybe their paths led them to a third person. Maybe they weren't the only women to disappear under similar circumstances. It was a long shot, but worth following up. And was Richard Wilson in Seabreak in 2000? It was something to consider.

She removed the photo of Adella from the manilla file and dropped it on the bedroom floor. Then she retrieved Jane's photograph and placed it beside the first picture. Standing over the images, Veronika noted something the two shared; they were both equally attractive. Attractive yet very different. Adella had dark hair and almost sensual lips while Jane was blonde and sweetly pretty. The biggest difference was the reticent look in Adella's troubled eyes.

Frustrated, she closed the file and picked up her phone.

"Did I wake you?" she asked.

She met Detective Allen Stewart of the Brisbane Missing Persons Unit a year ago while working on the Malicourt case. Soon after those mostly work-related phone calls, Veronika broke her one cardinal rule about dating cops and entered a long-distance relationship with the man. She'd also picked up Allen's habit of launching into a conversation without a greeting.

"No, I was thinking about you," he replied.

Just hearing his voice made her smile.

"I'm sure you were," she said. "But this is business – strictly."

"Okay," Allen replied. "Give me a minute and I'll put my uniform on."

"You don't wear a uniform." She chuckled, already knowing where he was heading.

"Now you're talking."

His voice was still husky from sleep. It was almost eleven o'clock in Queensland and she could imagine him up on one elbow, hair tousled and bleary-eyed.

"Don't try to distract me. I need to ask you something."

"Okay," he said with a touch of playfulness still in his voice.

She gave him a brief outline of the case, leaving out the names but including her belief that the two women were part of the same puzzle.

"So, what I want to know is, did you ever have a missing person who led to another missing person? Two people at the same time in the same place and then they both disappeared at different times?"

She was well aware of how strange the question sounded when said out loud. Yet the connection was there. She just needed to bounce the idea off someone who wasn't part of the case. And who better than a man who spent his life dealing with missing people?

There was a pause, silence on the end of the line. Maybe Allen was trying to think of a gentle way to tell her she was way off.

"Yes," he replied, and all trace of humour was gone. "About eight years ago, I had something like that. A missing girl. Nice kid, or at least that's what everyone said. Fifteen years old, from a decent home and then one day, she doesn't come home from school. I worked the case. The usual stuff, talking to friends, family and teachers and something came up. About a month before she went missing, Ella went on a school trip to this thing called Art in the Park."

Veronika thought she'd misheard him. "Sorry, Allen, did you say art?"

"You know, one of those temporary art exhibitions where all these artists set up their work. Anyway," he continued, "when Art in the Park came up, it got me thinking about a case from the year before. Not my case. One of the other guys in the unit's job. A girl who went missing on her way home from the art show."

"A connection," Veronika said around a surprised exhale. "What happened?"

"We questioned the artists and organisers, of course. Three were at both events. This one guy, a real hipster, turned out he had a prior arrest for attacking a woman back in art school. Hang on," he said, sounding hoarse, "I need a drink of water."

She heard the rustle of sheets. A few seconds later, Allen was back.

"The guy was a real creep. The sort that makes your skin crawl. We got a warrant and searched his place. We brought him in for questioning, but he was a smartass, wouldn't say a word. After that, the case stalled. But there was a connection between those girls, I–"

"Could feel it," she finished for him.

"Yes," he agreed. "I could feel it. But feelings don't solve cases."

She knew exactly what came next and part of her wished she'd never asked about the case because there were only a few ways the story could end and she could tell by his voice that none of them were going to be with good news.

"We didn't have the resources to watch him, so God knows how many of these art shows he does. I drive by his house every now and again and watch him climbing into his car." It seemed like there was more, but he stopped.

She wanted to say something comforting. Tell him he'd done everything he could, and the guy would make a mistake and Allen would be there when he did. But they'd both seen too much to believe tragic stories turned into happy endings.

"Sounds to me," he added, "like you've got something similar on your hands. A predator who knows how to cover his tracks."

"Looks like," she agreed.

They talked for a few more minutes, chatting about Allen's next visit to Perth. When she hung up, she should have called it a night, but Veronika was still thinking about the Jane Wilson case.

While her primary focus had to be Jane, there was something in Adella's eyes that spoke to her. If she had to name that something, she'd say fear. Was Adella a place to start? If so, who better to begin with than the woman's husband?

She was still pondering the possibility of a link between Adella and Jane when her phone rang.

"Sorry to call this late," Brian began. "I was going to wait until the meeting tomorrow–"

"It's fine," Veronika said, trying to keep the impatience out of her voice. "What's up?"

When she hung up, Veronika picked up Adella's photo. The ticking sensation in her mind kicked up a notch, and she felt the now familiar sense of urgency.

* * *

By the time everyone was seated, it was 8:30 a.m. After the phone conversation with Brian the night before, she'd had trouble sleeping. Not unusual when a case started to pick up speed, especially this early in an investigation. And her recent promotion from Senior Sergeant to Inspector gave her more autonomy over the investigations taken on by the Special Crime Squad.

The year before, riding the wave of success that came with closing the Malicourt case, Veronika had been offered the opportunity to make a swift ascent through the ranks by taking the exam to become Superintendent. An offer that was flattering, but ultimately one she turned down in favour of a position that would allow her to remain in the field and to really delve into cases and lead them in the way that she saw fit. However, the greater autonomy also came with other duties that competed for her time – in-depth meetings with Superintendent Grayson. A closer working relationship with a man who had resented her for years only made worse by the knowledge that she'd voiced her opinion and declared the role of superintendent was a desk job. A job that would take her away from the real business of solving cold cases. And she'd gone over his head to the assistant commissioner and asked to be assigned the Jane Wilson case.

Until Grayson retired or applied for a position outside of the Special Crime Unit, Veronika was stuck answering to a man who would delight in her spectacular failure on a high-profile case. An added pressure invading her thoughts as she tried to switch off and sleep.

"Leading up to the trip to Seabreak, Jane Wilson was anxious," Jim began, addressing the squad. "Makes sense. She was meeting her new in-law; her husband's twin brother. But, according to Jane's mother, there was more to it than nerves."

He turned to the screen behind him and clicked on his tablet and an image appeared; the newspaper article Haru found in the storage unit.

"Haru performed a search last night, and he is satisfied that this report didn't come from a major newspaper. Best guess is a local paper, but Haru's following that up today."

Haru nodded. "I've got a number for the *Seabreak Weekly*. Once it's confirmed as part of their publication, I'll try to access the publication date and any follow-up reports."

"As you can see," Jim continued, "the story details the case of a woman, Adella Reece, who went missing in Seabreak in 2000. We know Jane Wilson was in Seabreak that year on a family holiday. She was fifteen. What we don't know is why Jane kept the article. Why did she hide it and hang onto it for fifteen years?" He paused and looked around the room.

"What's the word in the margin?" Stacey asked. "Is it a word?"

"Could be a name," Brian offered.

Veronika, sitting to the side, stood and pointed to the scrawl. "The *D* is clearly discernible, but the rest is little more than a smudge."

"Could be meaningless," Stacey said. "Just a doodle she made while reading the piece."

"Could be," Brian replied, "but I don't think so."

Veronika span around, more than a little taken aback by how closely Brian's words echoed her own thoughts. She stared at him for a second, eyes narrowed and head tilted to the side. Usually the voice of flat facts. His willingness to follow a feeling surprised her.

"What's your take on it, Brian?" Veronika asked.

He furrowed his brow. "She kept it because it meant something to her. It meant something, so she wouldn't just doodle on it. The word means something."

As he spoke, Veronika found herself nodding.

"And," he continued, "it can't be a coincidence that the woman in the article, the article Jane kept, disappeared from the same town where Jane later disappeared. I don't buy it. Too far a reach."

"If there is a connection between Jane Wilson and Adella Reece," Veronika said, turning back to the screen and staring at the article, "we need to find it. I want an itemised list of everything you took from Jane's storage unit. And we need to verify the exact date in 2000 when

Jane's family visited Seabreak. We also need to speak to Adella's husband."

"Haru," Veronika said, turning to the detective constable. "When you're done with the local newspaper, I want you to do some digging. Find out if any other women went missing or reported being followed or attacked. Look for instances between Jurien Bay and Two Rocks over the last twenty years. Depending on what you find, we can broaden the search."

"Brian, Stacey," Veronika said to the remaining team members, "go see Jane's parents and ask them to confirm the dates they were in Seabreak. See if you can track down those parking stubs. Find out where Jane was going every two weeks leading up to her disappearance. The parents might be able to shed some light."

Veronika nodded to Jim. "We'll take a trip to Seabreak and talk to Adella's husband." She turned to Brian, who was already opening his laptop. "Can I see you in my office?"

* * *

"Sit down, Brian," Veronika said, gesturing at the chair and taking her seat on the opposite side of the desk.

"I have the itemised list ready. I can get a copy to you right away," Brian said, still standing.

"Thanks, but that's not why I wanted to speak to you," Veronika replied. "Sit."

"What you said out there" – Veronika nodded to the door – "about the word on the clipping, and I do believe it's a word or a name, meaning something, I know you explained yourself, but I think there's more. I asked for your thoughts on the article, but I don't think you told me everything."

Brian let out a long breath and shifted in his seat. "It's just a feeling, nothing concrete."

"I'd still like to hear it." She pushed.

"The clothes," he began. "Jane's clothes in the storage unit. They were expensive-looking, bright and colourful, but something about them didn't gel." Again, he looked uncomfortable. "I took one of her CDs. I mean, I put it on the list, but I took it home so I could listen to it."

He waited, and she could see he was expecting her to admonish him for removing the CD. Instead, she said, "Do you believe the CD is evidence?"

"No, I was hoping it would help clarify my impression about the clothes."

"And did it?" Veronika asked, genuinely curious.

"It might have been that she had music for every mood, but the singer – Nina Simone, I think was her name – she sounded mature, sad; I just got the impression that choosing to listen to that sort of music said something about Jane's state of mind." He gave her a pained look. "It's nothing solid, I know, and it won't cloud my judgement. If I have to, I'll go back to the storage unit and keep looking until I find something." He spread his hands wide. "If I'm wrong about Jane's state of mind, I won't hesitate to admit it."

Veronika almost smiled. "I'm pleased to hear that. I don't have to tell you that the facts and the evidence have to form the basis for any conclusions we draw. But don't discount your gut *or* be reluctant to include it in your theories."

He was nodding until the last part. She could see he was surprised by what she'd said.

"Getting a feel for people, dead or alive, victim or suspect, is something we do without consciously trying," she continued. "Over time, those instincts get sharper or become jaded, depending on what type of cop you become. *My* gut tells me yours falls in the first category."

"Huh." He looked relieved.

She tucked a strand of blonde, jaw-length hair behind her ear. "It doesn't matter how long you've been doing this; you can still get it wrong but it helps to be open to the little things. Minor details sometimes turn out to be the nail on which the whole case hangs. All I'm trying to say is, now they are open, don't close those doors."

She could see by his expression this wasn't how he'd thought the conversation would go, so she added, "If you're way off, I'll be the first to point it out."

"Okay." He drew the word out.

"Now," Veronika said, picking up her phone. "I have a meeting with Superintendent Grayson."

As Brian stood and headed for the door, she stopped him. "When the case is closed, put the CD back."

Chapter Twelve

The meeting went longer than Veronika expected, but it wasn't the only surprise Superintendent Grayson had in store for her. By 11:00 a.m., Veronika requested a few moments' break so she could text Jim and tell him their plan for the day had changed – drastically.

"Who tipped him off?" Jim asked when she returned to her office to find him waiting. "How could Richard Wilson know?"

"I don't know, but someone talked," Veronika replied. "The squad has only reached out to a few people. I'll bet my superannuation it was the friend, Caitlin Matthews. Certainly not Culla or Jane's parents. But the Grayson thinks the leak came from within the squad."

"That's rubbish," Jim snapped.

Veronika let out a tired sigh. "I know, but he's insisting I conduct an unofficial inquiry. He could barely keep the smug smile off his face when he told me."

"There goes our day," Jim replied.

"That's not all," Veronika continued. "Richard Wilson wants to talk to us; with his solicitor present, of course."

Jim steepled his fingers. "Maybe something good has come out of this mess. We need to question him at some point; this could be our best chance."

She had been thinking along the same lines. The circumstances were less than ideal and certainly not as she would have liked them, but they were going to have an opportunity to do something no one else had come close to in six years; have a face-to-face meeting with the man suspected of getting away with murder. Ideally, she'd like to have had more time to prepare. To gather more background information on Jane Wilson and dig deeper into the Adella Reece case. But the meeting was set for later that afternoon, and Veronika's time leading up to it was to be spent questioning her squad.

"We need to be ready," Veronika said. "We have to make this count."

"We will," Jim assured her.

"Hm," Veronika replied. "But first, I have to go through with this bogus inquiry. So, the sooner I start…"

Jim stood. "Who's the first lucky candidate?"

"Easy," Veronika said. "Did you tell anyone about the case being reopened?"

She tried to make the question sound light-hearted, but they both knew his answer would have to be recorded.

"No," Jim replied sombrely. "I haven't discussed the Wilson case with anyone outside of the squad, apart from Sergeant Bob Culla."

It was clear where Jim was pointing and it wasn't at any of her people.

"Good enough," she responded. "Could you send Stacey in?"

Each time she asked the question, the answer was the same. Yet, just saying the words felt like a betrayal of her team's trust. All she could hope was that the inquiry wouldn't undermine their faith in her. Damn Grayson, he had to know something like this could fracture the squad. Maybe that's why he'd forced her to be the one doing the interrogating. If the meeting with Richard Wilson went south, she had no doubt Grayson would throw her and the entire team under the bus.

* * *

At 2:45 p.m. Veronika and Jim made the short journey to Richard Wilson's apartment on Riverside Drive. With the afternoon sun rippling off the river and reflecting onto the glass and stone building, the perfect location screamed luxury.

"I'll take the lead," Veronika said once they were inside the lift. "But jump in if it feels right."

There was a line of perspiration gathering on the small of her back that had nothing to do with the outside heat or the bulk of her jacket. She had a plan, but the meeting with the Grayson and everything that followed had left her with no time to flesh that plan out. Essentially, she would be flying by the seat of her pants and when the stakes were high, that was never a good idea.

"You've conducted interviews under far worse circumstances," Jim replied, most likely sensing her unease. "The only difference here is the flash apartment and the subject's litigious nature."

As she agreed, Veronika found herself thinking of Len Davidson, an elderly man she met during the Malicourt case from the previous year. Len once gave her advice about cracking a tough case; *just keep asking questions until you get the right answers*. Perhaps that was all she could do; approach Wilson as she would any subject in an investigation and ask the hard questions. She'd never get answers if she let the AC's warnings throw her off her game.

Wilson greeted them with surprising politeness, given the circumstances. When he showed Veronika and Jim through to the kitchen and introduced them to his solicitor, Anton Seabber, Wilson even went as far as offering them tea or coffee. Something as mundane as drinking tea could help create an atmosphere that was less formal and felt more like a chat than an interrogation, so Veronika accepted his offer. She also wondered if Wilson was one step ahead of them and knew exactly what sort of scene *he* was setting.

"Mr Wilson," Veronika began, once they were seated around the kitchen table, "how did you know we were reopening the case?"

It was a blunt opening. But Superintendent Grayson had told her that he had received a call from Wilson and had no choice but to confirm that the case was being reopened. Their cards were well and truly on the table, so there was no point sticking to the routine review story. Veronika also knew that by being forthright, she was taking control of the conversation.

"Is that relevant?" Seabber, Wilson's solicitor, asked.

Veronika had heard of Anton Seabber. She'd seen him exiting the magistrates' offices a few times, but never actually spoken to the man. What she did know was that he had a reputation for being a razor when it came to cross-examining prosecution witnesses.

When Veronika replied, she addressed Wilson. "Yes, it is. If we are to have a frank conversation, it's something we need to be aware of."

"The manager of the storage unit, where my wife's possessions are kept, told me there had been a visit from the police," Wilson replied. "As Jane's next of kin, I thought you might have informed me that the case was being re-examined."

Where my wife's possessions are kept. Veronika picked up on a hint of bitterness on the word *kept.* Jane's parents had been very vocal in their belief that Richard Wilson had murdered their daughter. It wasn't surprising that the man harboured animosity towards the Campions. Still, the word *kept* sparked Veronika's interest.

"How do you feel about the case being reopened?" she asked.

"My client is fully supportive of any genuine attempts to discover what happened to his wife," Seabber again replied on his client's behalf.

"And we are trying to do just that," Veronika said, taking a sip of her tea. "So, we would be grateful for your cooperation."

Wilson, wearing spectacles and looking thin and a good deal older than the man who had appeared at the defamation trial six years earlier, was unreadable, so she continued.

"But there is one thing I need to know before we start." Veronika held Wilson's gaze. His eyes didn't flicker, but his shoulders stiffened.

"What do you think happened to your wife?"

Judging by his look of confusion, this wasn't the question he'd braced himself for.

"I think," Wilson said slowly, "she was abducted" – he let out a breath – "and murdered."

"Why would that be the case?" she asked, genuinely curious. "She might have decided to walk into the ocean. She wouldn't be the first." Veronika realised she was repeating Bob Culla's statement about Adella Reece.

"No," Wilson replied, sounding adamant. "That last night, Jane was making plans. She wanted us to buy a house." Just for a second, his eyes travelled to the picture window and the view of the Swan River. "There's no way she would have just changed her mind and killed herself. No way."

His candour impressed her. After everything that happened when his wife went missing, Veronika had expected anger, resistance, or perhaps flat-out disdain.

"We're trying to piece together your wife's movements in the weeks leading up to her disappearance," Veronika said, pushing on. "Who she saw, if anything out of the ordinary happened. Anything you can tell us would help."

When Wilson didn't respond, she continued. "Did Jane mention anything unusual happening in the lead up to your trip to Seabreak? Anyone hanging around? Say someone from her past? An old boyfriend?"

Again, Wilson turned to gaze out at the river. Now forty-three, the afternoon sun streaming in highlighted the deep lines on his face and his thinning hair, giving him the appearance of a man old beyond his years. Guilt could ravage a person both inside and out, but so could grief. So far, Veronika hadn't formed an opinion as to which burden had worn Richard's appearance down.

"She was anxious," Wilson finally replied. "I'd never seen her so nervous. I thought it was about meeting Edward, my brother, but when we arrived in Seabreak, she said something about seeing ghosts from her past.

"I should have pushed her, asked what she meant, but I made a joke of it." He closed his eyes. "If I could go back in time, I'd do things differently." He gave a joyless laugh. "Going back in time is all I do. I go over and over that day. If I'd just asked her what she meant instead of making a stupid joke. If I'd listened to her, let her explain, things would have been different. Jane would still be here if I turned the car around and went back to Perth."

The table they shared was small, almost too small, in the large kitchen dining room. Despite the expensive tiled floors, granite bench tops and spectacular view, the apartment felt sparse. A cold empty husk without the trappings and general clutter of a home. A cell-like place where the only colour came from the outside world. How many lonely nights, she wondered, had Richard spent reliving the hours leading up to his wife's disappearance? Or perhaps he knew exactly what happened to Jane, and the apartment was his form of self-imprisonment?

"Ghosts from her past," Jim asked, taking up where Veronika left off. "Did she mention anyone by name?"

Wilson shook his head as his eyes shifted towards his solicitor. Veronika got the feeling that this was a signal for the other man to intervene.

"In your initial report in 2015," Veronika jumped in before Anton Seabber could intercede, "you mentioned being worried because you'd had a strange conversation with Jane in the early hours of the day she disappeared. Can you be more specific? What did she say that had you so worried?"

Wilson ran his finger back and forth over his wrist, just above the watchband. "I can't remember," he said. "I just had the impression she was afraid of something."

"Of what?" she asked, leaning forward. "Did she mention visiting Seabreak as a teenager?"

Wilson's head snapped up, and his lids fluttered. "Look, I've told you what I know–"

"Alright," Seabber interjected. "Richard has been more than helpful." He took out his business card and pushed it across the table in Veronika's direction. "From this point on, questions go through me and I'd like you to keep me updated on the investigation. As Jane's next of kin, my client has a right to know what progress is being made."

She could see that persisting was useless. More questions at this point might risk fracturing the tenuous connection she hoped she'd made with Wilson.

"Of course." Veronika picked up the card and slipped it into her pocket. "I appreciate you taking the time to talk to us. We'll be in touch."

Before standing, she reached into her back pocket and produced her own card. Instead of handing it to the solicitor, she offered it to Wilson. "Sorry it's a bit crushed, but if there's anything else you think of?"

To her surprise, Richard Wilson nodded and took the card.

* * *

"What do you think?" she asked Jim when they reached the underground parking lot and walked towards their car.

"He's hiding something. At the very least, holding something back. But do I think he murdered her?" Jim shrugged. "That's the million-dollar question."

Once they were in the car, Veronika said, "When I asked him about the specifics of his last conversation with his wife, Richard started rubbing his finger over his wrist." She demonstrated, using her right index finger and running it over her left wrist. "He was self-soothing, trying to calm and ground himself. Something about that question alarmed him. He's holding something back and my bet is on his wife's connection to Seabreak. He knows something."

Chapter Thirteen

Same faces, same voices, same people crammed together with the stench of pizza and stale beer. It repulsed her. She'd spent too many nights in this pub and too many mornings regretting ever setting eyes on the place, yet she always came back. Now all Ashley wanted was out.

Pushing through the bodies to the cries of outraged punters telling her to watch what she was doing, she headed for the exit.

"Where are you going?" Evan's fingers dug into her bare arm.

Refusing to let him hold her back, she shook off his grip and kept moving. Outside, the warm night air offered little reprieve from the heat of the bar.

"I saw you in there." He'd followed her outside, and now his voice echoed off the flat slab of the parking lot. "You were all over that bloke," he continued, matching his pace to hers. "I know who he is. I know you've been seeing him behind my back."

When she refused to stop or answer, he grabbed the back of her neck. "You made me look like an idiot," he spluttered.

"Get the fuck off me," Ashley hissed, and twisted her head away from his sloppy fingers.

One night together, that's how long it took for Evan to decide he owned her, body and mind. Worse, he also seemed to think she owed him something. Five minutes of unsatisfying grunting, his not hers, in his rancid bed, and now she needed his permission to talk to another guy. When would she ever learn?

"What did you think this was, Evan?" she asked, stepping out of his reach. "Did you think we were going to get married? Did you think it was true love?"

She didn't like the hard edge to her voice, but it was the only language men like him understood.

"I thought..." He swayed and smacked his hand to his forehead. "Why do you have to be such a bitch?"

There were tears in his eyes, big wet drunken tears. In Ashley's experience, alcohol-addled tears could go one of two ways, violence or a breakdown, so she softened her tone. "Just go back inside and have a drink, okay?"

When he hesitated, she added, "I'll call you tomorrow."

She had no intention of calling – ever. But the promise seemed to calm the situation and in response, Evan nodded sleepily and turned. The list of men she would never call again was growing. Pretty soon there would be no one under fifty years of age in town whom she didn't have to cross the road to avoid. Did that say something about small-town life or about her as a human being?

There was a cluster of people around a hotted-up ute on the far side of the parking lot. The group, mostly guys, were too young to be served in the bar or to be of any interest to Ashley. Still, the whistles and hoots as she passed by were a confidence boost.

Why, she wondered, did she care what a bunch of seventeen-year-olds thought of her looks. After tonight, she'd change all that. Evan was a new low, even for her. God, she couldn't let herself sink any lower, could she?

Ashley touched the earrings Evan had bought her. Cheap, cutesy, dangling hearts. Like they were in love. Like he thought the crappy trinkets meant something. When she got home, she'd toss them in the rubbish bin. Even in her own mind, she sounded like a bitch. It wasn't Evan's fault; it was hers. In his own way, he'd tried. And what had she done in return? Rub his nose in the fact that she didn't want him. But surely there had to be something better than this life.

It was late, almost midnight, when she stepped out of the parking lot's lights and onto the coast road. She cursed herself for not bringing her own car in favour of letting Evan drive. Still, it wasn't an unpleasant walk, a bit lonely, but time to think was a good thing. Time to plan the changes she'd been dreaming about, but until tonight, hadn't taken seriously.

With the last echoes from the car park dying behind her, she pulled out her phone. Getting out of Ledge Point would be the first task, so why not start now and check on realestate.com for rentals in Perth. There were plenty of jobs. Hell, businesses state-wide were crying out for bodies to fill any number of positions. She was a hard worker and a fast learner. Maybe she'd even take some courses. A beauty therapy course, for instance.

A woman Ashley followed on YouTube had done the same sort of course before making a living doing wedding make-up. Now she was a full-time influencer with two hundred thousand followers and a sports car.

Ashley hadn't done well at school, but she was no idiot. That kind of success took work, and that was okay with her. Besides, she'd never get anywhere wasting her life at the local pub, falling into bed with anything with a pulse. Not for the first time, she asked herself, why? Why did she repeat the same mistakes over and over again? Sex addiction? A need for attention? She smiled to herself. Maybe she should study psychology and really figure herself out. Whatever the reason for her self-destructive behaviour, Evan was a long overdue wake-up call.

"Bugger," she muttered. "Of course, there's no signal." She chuckled at her own craziness.

There was never a signal on this patch of road. What did she expect? A small town like Ledge Point to suddenly burst into the twenty-first century?

The sound of her laughter reverberated in a strange way. Almost as if another noise had tacked itself onto the echo. She looked over her shoulder, half certain she'd see Evan hurrying to catch up to her. There was nothing, only the bushes and the road, turned into a soft blur by the partial moonlight.

An icicle of fear touched the base of her neck as the warm breeze tousled her hair. If there was a sound, it was probably rabbits. By night, the dunes were swarming with the little buggers. Stupid to be so startled by a rabbit. Even stupider to put herself in a situation where she had to walk home alone this late.

Ashley rubbed the back of her neck and walked on. Another five minutes and she'd round the bend into an area where houses overlooked the ocean. To a place where windows threw out light and the flat sound of the wind would be replaced by the comforting noise of blaring TVs.

It was almost funny to be so spooked. She'd laugh about it when she got home. She'd laugh her ass off, but not until she cleared the godawful stretch of road because right now, it felt like she was the only living thing in the world – apart from the rabbits. Only she wasn't alone because there was another *clack* behind her; the sound that a heel might make hitting the road.

Her breath dried in her mouth and instead of the pounding of the waves, all she could hear was blood rushing in her ears. What if she turned and looked back? What if there was someone behind her, grinning and stalking her like she was an animal? What then?

What then; the words catapulted her into a run. A sudden burst of speed that went no further than three paces before heavy hands grasped her, covering her mouth and lifting her off her feet.

Branches tore at her skin, and she had the sense that she was falling. She landed on her stomach with a bone-jarring thud. Mouth no longer covered, she tried to scream, but her face was pushed into the ground and she tasted sand on her lips.

Blind with panic, she struggled to crawl forward, only to have the air knocked out of her lungs when a crushing weight dropped onto her back. The world became darkness, grunting breaths on top of her and the feel of grit in her mouth. Hands gripped her neck, and she managed a strangled croak as sand invaded her nostrils.

The unbearable pressure on her throat intensified. As her eyes bulged, red sparks filled her vision.

"Slut. You always do this." The words barely registered.

Ashley was no longer aware of what she was doing as her fingers clawed at the sand. A few seconds later, the world turned black.

Chapter Fourteen

"This is good," Veronika said, leafing through the printed pages. She checked her watch; 9:05 a.m. "We have time for a short briefing before DS Drommel and I leave for Seabreak. I want you to run the team through what you've found before we go over our next move."

"Um…" Haru shifted in his seat.

She could see he was reluctant to address a team of detectives who outranked him. Haru had been with the squad for over a year. Junior officer or not, he had to get used to standing behind his work. So far, he'd showed a keen eye for sifting through data and pinpointing critical information.

"You'll be fine," she continued. "Your research is solid. Just trust your instincts. If you're off, someone will point it out. Take the criticism on the chin. It comes with the territory."

She took a sip of tea from her mug and noticed the list of items taken from Jane Wilson's storage unit sitting beside her computer. Knowing Brian must have left it for her, she grabbed the list, folded it and slipped it in the inside pocket of her jacket.

Ten minutes later, Haru stood in front of the squad.

"I ran a search using certain parameters," he began. "Missing women and girls aged between sixteen and fifty years, between 2000 and 2020, focusing on the one hundred-and-sixty-eight-kilometre area between Jurien Bay and Two Rocks.

"I was able to narrow the search by disregarding women whose bodies were recovered and foul play was ruled out. That leaves us with Adella Reece in 2000, Jane Wilson in 2015, both disappeared from Seabreak and Candice Burns in 2007, who was last seen in Ledge Point." He touched his tablet and the screen behind him displayed a report dated March 12th, 2007.

"Candice Burns disappeared while walking home from a friend's house in 2007. There had been some sort of argument between Candice and her friend over the friend's boyfriend. Candice left the house in tears and was last seen walking towards the coast road. There was an investigation and a public appeal but the case stalled," Haru concluded.

"The boyfriend, the one the friends argued about?" Brian asked.

"He didn't leave the house," Haru replied. "There were a few other people at the residence who verified that the friend and her boyfriend were still present when the get-together wound up at around midnight. The couple alibied each other, saying they spent the night together."

Haru clicked, and the next image appeared on the screen. A pretty young woman with red hair, smiling and holding what looked like a glass of wine. Like Jane and Adella, Candice was a knockout. The three women had one thing in common: their good looks. A coincidence? From her chair at the side of the room, Veronika thought not.

The only difference between the three women, Adella, Jane, and Candice, as far as Veronika could see, was time and money. Jane was independently wealthy, with affluent parents. Adella and Candice were run-of-the-mill, small-town women. Their disappearances wouldn't have made a big splash in the media. But, social standing aside, all three had to have someone who grieved their loss.

"When she disappeared, Candice was twenty-three years old. This photo was taken shortly before she vanished," Haru continued. "I'm still following up on reported attacks or recorded incidents of women being followed, but there's quite a bit to get through."

"What do we know about Candice?" Veronika asked.

Haru glanced at his tablet. "One arrest for drunk and disorderly in 2006. Only child. Her parents live in Ledge Point."

"Who was the arresting officer?" Veronika asked.

"A Constable Able Martin," Haru replied. "But the charge was dropped."

Veronika thought for a moment. Candice's arrest would have been during Culla's time in the region. She made a mental note to call the sergeant and ask if he had any involvement in Candice's arrest or if he'd taken the initial report when she went missing.

"Ledge Point," Stacey said. "That's not far from Seabreak."

"Travelling at a modest seventy kilometres per hour, it would take around forty-three minutes to drive from Seabreak to Ledge Point," Haru replied.

There were a few seconds of silence as everyone absorbed what Haru had said.

"Thanks, Haru," Jim said, stepping to the head of the room. Then, turning his attention to Brian, he asked, "Anything on the parking stubs you found in Jane's glovebox?"

From his seat, Brian checked his notes. "Jane's parents confirmed their daughter had been seeing a psych, Dr Albian Sharm. His office is in the building next to the parking lot address on the ticket stubs. Apparently, Jane had been seeing the psych on and off for about four years. Although the mother did seem surprised that Jane had started seeing him again in the months before she disappeared."

"Get a warrant," Jim replied. "We need to see his notes and find out why Jane was back to regular visits. But talk to the psych before you serve it. Confidentiality survives the death of a patient, but under the circumstances he should be willing to cooperate."

Jim nodded to Stacey. "Where are you with the dates on Jane Wilson's family holiday in Seabreak?"

"When Brian and I spoke to her yesterday, Jane's mother was sure it was in January or early February. Sometime after New Year's Eve, but before school holidays ended. She's going to have a look through some photo albums and see if she can find pictures with dates."

"Spoke to someone at the *Seabreak Weekly*," Haru put in. "The Adella Reece article went out on the twentieth of January 2000."

From memory, Veronika knew Adella vanished on the 18th of January 2000. If Marian Campion was correct about the dates, that might put Jane in Seabreak when Adella disappeared. Experience had taught her that random coincidences were rarely as random as they seemed.

"And the ex-boyfriend?" Jim asked.

"The parents knew she was seeing someone before she met Richard, but they never met him and Jane wouldn't give them a name." Before anyone could comment, Stacey continued. "Jane's mother said she was always quite secretive about her relationships. They only knew of Richard a few weeks before the wedding. I'm trying to get hold of Caitlin, Jane's old roommate. I had a feeling she was holding back about the ex, but she's not picking up."

Jim nodded. "Okay. If you can't get anything from the roommate, chase up some of the people Jane worked with at Avenue Theatre. Maybe she confided in someone there."

Stacey nodded and wrote in her notebook.

"For now," Jim continued, "Jane Wilson is our chief priority. DI Pope and I will interview Adella's husband, talk to the local cops, and chase up any leads in Seabreak. See if there is a connection between the two women. And with any luck, Edward Wilson will agree to speak to us." He glanced at Veronika and she could see he was waiting for her to close the briefing.

"I've closed the inquiry into the source of the information leak. The storage unit manager was on Richard Wilson's payroll. As far as I'm concerned, the matter is closed." She stood and took a second before continuing. "I know it wasn't pleasant, but the questions had to be asked."

Looking around, she could see the faces of her team members. They weren't happy and for that, she couldn't blame them. Not for the first time, she wondered if accepting the promotion to Inspector was really what she wanted.

"I'll be passing my findings on to Superintendent Grayson, as well as my formal objection to the knee-jerk reaction geared towards internal blame." Veronika planted her hands on her hips. "I know this was a kick in the guts, but it had to be done. All we can do is move on and focus on the case, so let's get going."

When the meeting broke up, she stopped by Brian's desk and saw that he was already working on the search warrant for Jane's medical notes. "Thanks for the list," she said and patted her jacket pocket.

"No worries, boss," he replied.

He seemed to want to say more, so she waited.

He sat back in his chair. "Jane and Adella in the same place at the same time, there's got to be more to it. If the timeline matches up, I don't believe it's a coincidence."

"Neither do I," she responded. "We'll be out of the office for the rest of the day. Keep me posted on the psych."

Chapter Fifteen

Brian had seen a psych himself, back when he was in uniform and new on the job. Mandatory visits following a fatal shooting were routine. It didn't matter that he wasn't the one who pulled the trigger. The department ordered counselling sessions for all officers involved in incidents where deadly force was involved.

At first, he resented the mandatory sessions. He'd seen a meth-head's brain spewed out on the filthy carpet in a cockroach-infested house. Wasn't that enough? The last thing he wanted was to rehash the gory details for some uni graduate who had never faced an angry man with an axe in his hands.

But the psych turned out to be anything but a fresh-faced graduate. Dasha Charlic was a fifty-something Hungarian woman with a smoker's rasp and a knack for cutting to the chase. No touchy-feely stuff, just questions. Questions that sliced to the heart of a problem that, at first, he didn't think he had. Then, when the dreams started, he was more than grateful that there was someone he could share them with. Someone like Dasha, who didn't offer platitudes or suggest meditation.

"You will live with these memories," she had said in her flat, gravelly voice. "Don't hide from them because they will find you. You must be ready for *them*."

And he was.

Albian Sharm's rooms were nothing like Dasha's stark office. Sharm's set up reeked of money. Dark leather, tranquil artwork and shuttered windows – the perfect setting for the wealthy to lament their pampered lives. An environment designed to add authenticity to their problems. Brian caught himself judging the people who frequented Sharm's practice and stopped. Rich or not, everyone had a right to be ready when the memories came. When the nightmares showed up.

"I'm happy to help," Dr Sharm said, gesturing for Brian to sit. "But I don't think there's much I can contribute."

There was a chesterfield couch and armchair facing the doctor's desk. Brian took the armchair.

"As I mentioned on the phone," Brian began, "this is just a routine review, something we do with all cold but still open cases."

The partially closed blinds behind Sharm's head let in bars of light, which cast shadows on the doctor's face. Raised a Catholic, Brian thought the effect was almost that of the confessional box. He wondered if this was a deliberate tactic on the doctor's part, to make himself appear as almost a shadow. A conduit to some greater force. Something he did to encourage his patients to speak freely and feel somehow anonymous.

"Well, I'm not sure what I can add to the review," Sharm reiterated. "But I'm happy to help within the boundaries of patient confidentiality."

There it was. He had been expecting the doctor to err on the side of caution and resist disclosure. Brian decided to wait on the search warrant and see if he could draw Sharm out.

"So, you were seeing her," Brian said as a statement, not a question.

The angle of the doctor's face made it difficult to tell, but Brian thought he saw the man's lids flutter. Was he searching his mind for information? Brian doubted it. Jane Wilson was a familiar name, a long-standing patient and a well-known missing person. Not to mention that Sharm had had all morning; knowing he was to receive a visit from police regarding Jane Wilson, it stood to reason that he would review his notes and bring his patient to mind. There was definitely something else in the doctor's reaction, so Brian waited.

"She was my patient, yes," Dr Sharm replied. "I treated her on and off for several years."

"Her father described her as sensitive. What do you think he meant by that?" Brian asked.

"Sensitive in some ways perhaps, but aren't we all?" he replied.

He was being evasive, so Brian moved on. "Did she ever mention being worried or afraid of someone?"

Sharm swivelled his chair to the right. "We discussed many things. If I thought she was in any danger, I would have reported my concerns to the police."

"But you didn't," Brian clarified.

"No, Detective, I didn't."

"Before Jane met her husband, did she confide in you about someone she was seeing? A boyfriend?" Brian asked. "Someone she'd had a relationship with? A relationship she ended abruptly?"

Sharm leaned forward and his face came into the light. Angular features, tanned skin and dark hair greying slightly at the temples; a face that might have been considered attractive.

"The things Jane disclosed are confidential, so I'm not at liberty to go into detail." He spread his hands wide. "As I say, if I thought she was in any danger, I would have had a professional and moral obligation to let the police know."

It was useless and there was something about the man that got under Brian's skin, but he wasn't ready to pull back yet. "What about Seabreak? Did she talk about her memories of the place?"

"I'm sorry, Detective, but I won't discuss the nature of my sessions with Jane."

"Fair enough," Brian replied, changing gears. "I have a search warrant which allows me to cease your files, notes and records as they pertain to Jane Wilson." It was petty, but he felt a second of satisfaction when the look of defiance ran away from the doctor's face.

"It would have been easier if you'd tried being frank," Brian pushed on. "Jane has been missing for seven years. Knowing what was troubling her might help us find her and bring closure to her family." He produced the document from his jacket pocket and slapped it on the desk.

At the sight of the warrant, the doctor's demeanour changed. "I'd like to read that," he said, snatching up the paper.

This wasn't how Brian had hoped the meeting would go, but it was clear the doctor was resistant to cooperating. Brian understood the doctor owed his patient protection. Some pushback was to be expected, but after seven years, they both knew Jane was dead. To Brian's mind, Sharm was being deliberately obtuse.

Brian waited while Dr Sharm turned on the desk lamp – no confessional anonymity now – and began reading the document.

An hour later, Brian gave Sharm a receipt and picked up two boxes of paperwork to take to his car. It would take hours, if not days, to go over every entry, so he intended to start as soon as he got back to the squad room.

As he left the doctor's rooms, Brian heard the man on his phone speaking in a hushed, animated tone. Brian's guess was he was talking to a solicitor. Maybe, he decided, it might be worth doing a bit of digging into Dr Albian Sharm.

Chapter Sixteen

Frustrated with calling and receiving no answer, Stacey drove to Caitlin's apartment. From what she'd gathered on her last visit, Jane's old roommate didn't go out much, so there was a good chance of catching her at home.

"Oh." Caitlin, wearing a pink terrycloth dressing gown and still holding the door, seemed more than a little surprised to find Stacey on her doorstep.

"I tried calling," Stacey said.

"I'm sort of busy and I'm expecting a delivery."

"It will only take a couple of minutes," Stacey replied, stepping forward.

Caitlin grudgingly held the door open and followed Stacey into the apartment. "I suppose it's okay, but I don't know what else I can tell you."

Still near the doorway, Stacey turned and stopped so abruptly Caitlin almost ran into her. While the woman was off balance and trying to put some space between them, Stacey asked, "Did you remember the name of the man Jane was seeing before Richard?"

"What?"

Stacey could see Caitlin heard exactly what she'd been asked and was playing for time.

"The man's name," Stacey pushed. "You couldn't think of it when I was last here. Did you remember?"

She knew she was being heavy-handed, but the roommate was dodging her calls and hiding something. Sometimes a little space invasion sent a message that words couldn't deliver. A message that implied the police were closing in and wouldn't take no for an answer.

Caitlin hesitated for a second and then sidestepped around Stacey.

"I can't remember everything that happened seven years ago," she mumbled and walked to the sofa.

It wasn't quite an invitation to stay, but since she hadn't come out and asked her to leave, Stacey followed her. Taking up the same position opposite the woman that she'd occupied two days before, Stacey tried a different approach.

"It must be nice working from home" – Stacey nodded to the window – "especially with the view."

If Caitlin was surprised by the change of direction, she didn't show it. "I used to love going out. Because Jane worked at the theatre, she could always get tickets to big events. Private parties and VIP dinners. That's how she met Richard, at a fundraiser hosted by his company," she replied, not really answering the question.

"You miss her," Stacey said.

She wasn't great at the soft approach, but Caitlin seemed to want to talk about happier times. A time when she and Jane were close. Perhaps reminding her of how important that friendship was might jog her memory.

"Yes, it's been a long time, but I miss her very much. When someone leaves your life so suddenly, it creates a void. I haven't done well at filling it." She tightened the cord on her dressing gown. "Sounds a bit pathetic when I say it out loud, doesn't it?"

The ginger cat stalked into the room and leapt onto the arm of Caitlin's sofa. As he settled himself, he regarded Stacey with suspicious yellow eyes.

"No," Stacey responded. "Not at all. She was your friend. None of us have enough of those."

She waited a beat as the woman swiped at the tears that were rolling down her cheeks. Upsetting someone as obviously fragile as Caitlin brought Stacey no joy. In fact, sometimes her job made her feel like a world-class asshole, but on the flip side, Jane's parents were living a nightmare. An endless stretch of days filled with grief and fading hope.

"I want to find her," Stacey said with sincerity. "For you and her family. But to do that, I need your help."

Caitlin was staring down at her hands. She knew more, but was still reticent.

"I know you're loyal to her. You want to protect her, but by telling me what you know, you're giving her a voice." She saw Caitlin's shoulders tremble, so she pushed on. "Someone took her voice away. Someone silenced her. This is your chance to speak for her."

"All right," Caitlin sobbed. "I don't know his name; I wasn't lying about that. But the rest, I don't suppose it's worth hiding anymore."

The first thing Stacey did when she left the apartment was call Brian.

Chapter Seventeen

They were on the road, heading south towards Seabreak. It was still early; just after ten o'clock, but the mercury was already on the rise and, despite the car's air con, the cab was stuffy. Veronika slipped off her jacket and tossed it on the back seat.

"How's the little one doing?" she asked Jim.

Until then, he'd been uncharacteristically quiet, but at the mention of his daughter, Amelie, he smiled.

"She took her first steps the other night. No hesitating, just up and on the go." He chuckled. "She's like her mother when she sets her mind to something." He made a forward gesture with his hand. "There's no stopping her. And Hope follows her around like a mother duck."

Hope, a golden retriever he'd rescued during a case a few years back, had become a part of Jim's family, so Veronika was happy to hear the dog was taking to life with a toddler in the house.

"You should come over for lunch," he continued. "Julie would love to see you."

"Just let me know when and I'll be there," Veronika replied. "The early days can be rough, but I remember how having a toddler has a way of putting life into perspective."

As they travelled along Indian Ocean Drive, the smell of salt from the ocean was carried on the breeze. "Enjoy it while you can," she continued. "I know it's a cliché, but time goes by so quickly. Those years when you're their entire world are irreplaceable."

"He's moving out then?" Jim asked. He didn't have to elaborate; they both knew he was talking about Tony.

"Yes," she replied, tipping her head back. "Verity is a nice kid, and he's happy. It will be good for him."

"But?" Jim asked, taking his eyes off the road for a second.

"There's no but, it's a good thing. The right thing. I just wish I was as ready for it as Tony seems to be," she responded. "It is what it is, though. But just so soon."

Before Jim could reply, Veronika's phone rang.

"Turns out Jane had a relationship with her psych," Brian said, not bothering with a greeting. A style of communication that seemed to be popular with male cops. "I don't know the details, but according to the roommate, they were seeing each other in a less than professional capacity when Jane met Richard. That's when she ended it with the psych. And," Brian continued, "the man has an enormous ego. He was steaming when I served the warrant."

Veronika thought for a moment. "Go through the files and notes. If Jane broke it off with the doctor, he might have reacted badly. Maybe he wasn't willing to let her go."

"I'm on it," Brian said and hung up.

"So," Jim said. "The doc might be in the frame. If Detective Bender hadn't been so blinkered, he might have found out about the relationship."

"Maybe," Veronika said, unconvinced. "It doesn't explain the link between Jane and Adella. Let's call in on Candice Burns's parents while we're in the area. Maybe there's something that links her to our other missing women."

* * *

Seabreak was a place in constant motion. The incessant sea breeze shifted the sands and twisted the trees. Despite the summer sun, there was a bite in the air when Veronika stepped out of the car and stretched her back muscles. She slipped on her jacket and winced at the stiffness in her shoulder.

A scrubby patch of parkland separated Jason Reece's house from the others on the street. A brittle-looking structure sitting on wooden struts, the home appeared tacked together. With the mid-afternoon light touching the building's front door, it struck Veronika as an isolated dwelling. The peeling remnants of pale blue paint spoke to the occupant's indifference to the home. Or, Veronika thought, it said something about the owner's refusal to make any changes and move on with his life. Did he still harbour hopes his wife would return?

Jim knocked on the front door, a steady double pound that carried the sound of authority. They waited a few beats for signs of movement before he knocked for a second time.

"Might be out," Jim offered.

Their visit was unannounced, so it was possible, but Veronika wasn't willing to give up and come back later just yet. Stepping to the right and over an upturned milk crate, she peered through the window. The room inside was in shadows, with no sign of movement. As she stepped back, Veronika noticed a fly on the windowpane. A second later, another landed and both insects crawled their way up the inside of the glass. She frowned and listened.

"What is it?" Jim asked.

"Do you hear that?" she replied.

He started to shake his head and then stopped. Buzzing, soft like a distant engine. As they spoke, a third fly landed on the glass.

Not needing to be told what Veronika suspected, Jim nodded. "I'll go this way," he said as he stepped off the porch and headed around the left side of the building.

Veronika's heart rate kicked up a notch as she moved to the right of the house. Any number of things could account for the flies. Rotten food, a dead animal or just unsanitary living conditions. She'd seen it before – people living in squalid conditions, their homes infested with flies, maggots, and cockroaches. The memory of those tragic homes made her skin crawl and her heart ache in equal measure. Still, there was something ominous in the hum that filled the air and seemed to come from everywhere and nowhere at the same time.

As she walked, she pushed back her jacket and tucked the tail into the back of her pants, allowing easy access to her gun. There was a window facing south, but too high up to be of any use. Further along was a tacked-on structure that jutted from the left side of the house, with a door and a small window.

Veronika ducked past the door and peered through the window. Grime and lack of lighting made it impossible to see. One thing was clear, the hum was louder here – almost frantic.

She used her forearm to swipe sweat from her brow and reached for the door. The knob turned, and the door swung inwards. The sound of furious insects almost obscured the rusty whine of the hinges. A fly landed on Veronika's cheek and she swatted at it with a disgusted grunt.

Once detected, the odour was unmistakable. A familiar smell which she recognised from bitter experiences. One of sweet, cloying rot and human waste. As she stepped into the building, the trapped heat forced the stench into her mouth and nostrils.

Trying to breathe through her mouth, she covered her nose with the crook of her arm and used her free hand to search for a light switch. It took a few seconds, but she found the switch only to click twice and discover it was useless.

"Damn it," she mumbled, and pulled out her phone.

Using one hand, she turned on the torch function and played the light around the room. With a workbench, shelves, crates, old lawn mowers and a mismatched collection of tools, the area appeared to be a workshop.

The light landed on an overturned stool. Even before she lifted the beam, Veronika knew what she would find. With her gut tensed, she looked up. A man, Jason Reece, she assumed, hanging from an overhead beam.

"Christ," she whispered and waved away another fly.

In the narrow shaft of torchlight, the man's face, crawling with flies, was turned a grotesque blue. Jason Reece was long dead. Veronika wasn't an expert, but judging by the insects and the smell, it had been at least a day or so. And, with the summer heat building up in the workshop, that was long enough to turn the scene into the stuff of nightmares.

She backed out of the workshop and put some distance between herself and the body. Enough space so that she could gulp in less tainted air.

Before acting, she closed her eyes and replayed the scene in her mind. The tragedy and humanity of the man's death left her off balance. What had driven him to such a desperate act of self-harm? No amount of experience could soften the impact of what she'd seen. Each time, and there had been many, she felt the familiar stab of grief for the stranger. With the grief also came relief. Relief that her humanity was still intact, and she hadn't lost her ability to care. It also reminded her that this was a job she loved – and sometimes hated.

Veronika texted Jim with a scant outline of what she'd discovered. She then called an ambulance. The man was beyond help, but that was the protocol and so was notifying the local police. As a senior detective, discovering the body meant that overseeing the investigation would fall to her. A complication in an already crowded investigation, but a necessary one.

Despite all the demands on her time, she would do her best not to pass off Jason Reece to another detective. She found the man; she would ensure his death was properly investigated. When Jim's footfalls pounded around the side of the house and he jogged past her and into the workshop, she was on the line with the Joondalup Forensic Unit.

"Forensics will be here in about an hour and a half," Veronika said to Jim when she hung up.

She was about to say more when her phone rang. "Superintendent Grayson," she said to Jim before taking the call.

Grayson didn't mince his words, just a brusque request for an update. Veronika turned and walked back to the open workshop door.

"We're making progress," she said, breathing in the smell of death. "We're in Seabreak interviewing witnesses. I'll have a full report for you at the meeting tomorrow."

"Jesus, Vee," Jim said when she hung up. "Was that smart?" He looked pale, but, she thought wryly, finding a flyblown corpse will do that.

"It gives us time," she replied. "Let's find some light. I want to look around before forensics shows up."

Jim retrieved paper shoe covers and gloves from the car. Once they were suited up, it took a few minutes shining their phone lights around to locate a couple of fishing lanterns in the workshop which they set up on the floor around the body.

"Search the house while I stay with the body," she said once the lights were in place. "We need to be sure this is Jason Reece, and he's not hiding somewhere in the house." She gestured over her shoulder in the house's direction. "Break a window if you have to. We don't know what we're dealing with here."

"Right," Jim said, removing his shoe covers. "I'll see if I can find a driver's license. Might help us confirm if that man *is* Reece."

"I don't like the timing on this," she replied, watching him in the doorway.

"Me neither," he said, before jogging towards the front of the house.

Once alone, Veronika stood before the body and took a second to ground herself. In this moment, she would give her whole mind to the deceased. The insects, the buzzing, the smell; she forced them to the background and concentrated on the details. By doing this, the substance of the scene became her focus.

Ready to begin, she used her phone and took a series of photographs. Images of the body, the overturned stool, and the workshop. Forensics would do the same, more in fact, only she didn't want to wait for their images. In the time it took for the forensic team to get their photos back to her, Veronika would study her own pictures.

Chapter Eighteen

"According to Dr Sharm, Jane Wilson suffered from panic attacks and paranoia," Brian said to Stacey.

They were in the squad room in Perth Central Police Station, the multi-storey building that housed the Homicide Division and the Special Crime Squad. The only other person in the room was Haru, working quietly with his back to them.

"Panic attacks," Brian read from the open file on his desk, "that the patient, Jane Wilson, first experienced in her teenage years. Sharm notes the cause of the attacks as trauma. God, this man is a bastard. A woman comes to him with these problems, and he starts a sexual relationship."

Stacey wheeled her chair over to Brian's desk and picked up one of the files.

"We'll get through these quicker if we divide them up," she said.

Brian was a self-contained man. Not one to ask for help, but in the year they'd worked together, Stacey found him to honest, to a fault sometimes, but always focused on the job. When he let the hard exterior slip, he was also a kind man. Still, it was the first time she'd ever seen him so passionate in his anger.

"Thanks," he replied with what might have been a smile. "Sharm makes copious notes. There's another stack." He pointed to a box on the floor next to his desk.

"A sleaze with a pen," Stacey said, opening the file. "This should be interesting."

An hour later, she ran her fingers through her short spiky hair and read over another page of Dr Sharm's scrawl. So far, all she'd discovered was that Jane had trouble sleeping because she experienced feelings of dread. Dread; the word reappeared numerous times. Further on, Stacey stopped and reread a single line.

> *Patient continues to experience feelings of dread and guilt.*

It was the first time the doctor had noted guilt and the word's sudden appearance had her thinking.

"Have you read anything about Jane feeling dread?" she asked Brian.

He nodded. "Dread and anxiety. I thought dread was a symptom of anxiety, but I'm no expert."

"What about guilt?" Stacey asked. "Anything?"

"Nothing, but guilt could be connected to her relationship with the doctor," he replied, putting sarcastic emphasis on the word *doctor*.

Stacey thought for a moment. "Could be, but is it strange that Sharm doesn't give any details? Like what was the source of Jane's dread? Or was it unnamed dread? Why doesn't he write about what triggered her anxiety and guilt? Apart from a vague reference to trauma, there are no details."

Brian flicked through his stack of files and pulled one to the top. "In Sharm's initial intake notes in 2010, he states that Jane had been in therapy for a year before she was hospitalised in 2006 for depression and anxiety. Again, no details," he said, closing the file.

"Surely, he would focus on the cause of her anxiety in order to treat her. Wouldn't it be essential for him to know why she felt guilt and dread?" Stacey asked. "It appears as though he's only recording part of the problem. Why would he do that?"

"Maybe," Brian said, turning to his computer, "we should ask him."

* * *

Albian Sharm's home address was easy to discover through a driver's license search. At 5:30 p.m., Brian and Stacey pulled up outside the man's home in City Beach.

"He might refuse to speak to us," Stacey said, watching the lighted windows on the doctor's double-storey house.

Modest compared to the homes on either side, the location alone would still put the price of Sharm's house at well over a million dollars. The man had a lot to lose if someone reported his relationship with Jane Wilson to The Psychology Board of Australia. Caitlin said Jane ended their relationship, but what if she'd done more than just break things off? What, Stacey wondered, would the doctor have done if Jane threatened to report his conduct to the board?

"I'm hoping a surprise visit to his home might get him talking," Brian replied, opening the car door.

Sharm answered on the second ring. On seeing them, the man's mouth dropped open, but Brian didn't give him a chance to speak.

"Sorry to disturb you," Brian began, not sounding in the least bit sorry. "We have a few questions about Jane Wilson. Can we come in?" He was already stepping forward when the doctor held up his hand, signalling Brian to stop.

"No, you can't," Sharm snapped, recovering some of his composure. "This is my home. You can't just show up here at any hour. Call my office tomorrow and–"

"Who is it, Al?" A woman's voice called from somewhere down the hall.

"It's a work thing," he replied, holding the door and turning his back on them. "I'll be right there."

"This is highly inappropriate," Sharm said, lowering his voice and addressing Brian. "Like I said, call my office."

He was about to close the door when Brian slapped his hand on the wood and prevented the doctor from shutting them out.

"Speaking of inappropriate," Brian said, "what was the exact nature of your personal relationship with Jane Wilson?"

A look crossed the man's face. One Stacey had seen countless times – shock, panic, and a rapid shuffling of emotions. Usually, that shuffle landed on anger.

"I don't know what you're talking about, but I don't like what you're implying," Sharm recovered quickly, but not quick enough. Stacey had clocked the panic and, judging by his restraining palm still on the door, so had Brian.

"I have a witness who claims Jane confided in her about an intimate relationship she shared with you. Because Mrs Wilson was your patient, if the allegation is true, we're bound to report it to The Psychology Board of Australia," Brian continued, raising his voice. "And this new information raises some questions about the events leading up to Mrs Wilson's disappearance."

"I… I don't," Sharm stammered and glanced over his shoulder.

"It's just a few questions," Stacey interjected, seizing the opportunity to play good cop. "We'd like to clear the matter up so we can move on with our investigation."

There was a pause while Sharm looked from Brian to Stacey. The doctor was a good ten centimetres taller than Brian, but it was clear her partner intimidated him.

"Okay," Sharm said. "Give me a minute."

The doctor disappeared into the house and pulled the door partially shut behind him. They heard voices, and Brian glanced in Stacey's direction. A minute later, the doctor reappeared.

"My study is this way." He gestured for them to follow him. "But make it quick. We're having guests for dinner."

The study was small, one wall was lined with books and the other decorated with framed diplomas and degrees. Sharm turned his chair away from his desk in the corner and sat with his arms folded. He didn't invite Stacey or Brian to do the same, so they remained standing.

Stacey noticed a photograph on the doctor's desk. A framed image of a woman who looked considerably younger than Sharm and a little girl. The child looked to be eight or nine years old.

"Nice photo," Stacey said, nodding towards the desk. "Your family?"

Sharm was wearing a short-sleeved shirt. When Stacey mentioned his family, the man tugged at one sleeve and nodded.

"My wife and daughter," he replied. "Can we hurry this up?"

"What did Jane feel guilty about? In your notes, you said she felt dread and guilt. Why?" Brian asked, without preamble.

Sharm gave an impatient shrug. "She struggled with depression and anxiety. If you knew anything about psychology, you'd understand that feelings of that nature are symptoms of a bigger problem."

"But she talked to you about more than just the symptoms, right?" Brian insisted. "Why did she feel guilty? Was it because of your personal relationship, or was it something else?"

Sharm was back to tugging his sleeve. "Look, you have it all wrong," he said. "Whatever she might have believed… It wasn't real–"

"Rubbish," Brian spat. "You knew she was fragile, and you pounced on her like a rat on a garbage can. What did she tell you?"

"I don't know." He looked around exasperated and leaned back in his chair. "I tried to get to the source of her fears, but there was always something she held back. I did what I could, but if a patient refuses to trust me, I can only do so much."

"She started seeing you again shortly before she disappeared," Stacey interjected. Her instincts told her Dr Sharm knew more than he was letting on and she intended to get to the truth. "Why did she come back?"

"It didn't make much sense. Initially, she said she was anxious about meeting her new brother-in-law, but the last time I saw her, she appeared to be deteriorating," Sharm replied. "I recommended she spend some time in a private facility, but she wouldn't hear of it. She said she was damned because of something she'd seen."

"What?" Brian asked. "What had she seen?"

The doctor rubbed his forehead. "It was nonsense. That's why I suggested going into a facility. I could see she was experiencing a break from reality."

"What did she say?" Brian asked. For the first time since the interview started, Stacey wasn't sure if the threat in her partner's voice was real or still part of the good cop, bad cop routine.

"She said," Sharm replied, sounding exhausted, "she'd seen someone being murdered."

"Okay," Brian said. "Where were you on February the 13th, 2015?"

* * *

They headed back to the squad room so Stacey could pick up her car. As they left the affluent beachside suburb and Dr Sharm's house behind, the setting sun was bleeding purple into the Indian Ocean.

“So, Jane tells her doctor that she witnessed a murder and, shortly after, she goes missing,” Brian said, pulling onto Cambridge Street. “And he never thought to mention it to the police. Patient confidentiality, my ass. Sharm didn’t want to draw attention to himself because he was afraid his dirty secret would come to light. And now he’s saying it all happened so long ago, he can’t remember where he was when she disappeared.

“A woman he had an intimate relationship with goes missing. It’s all over the news and Sharm can’t remember anything about where he was when it happened. I’m calling bullshit on this.”

“Or he’s lying through his teeth; trying to deflect blame onto some mysterious murderer. Sharm’s daughter, the one in the picture, has to be at least nine years old,” Stacey said.

Brian frowned, but didn’t take his eyes off the road. “So Sharm wasn’t only married when he was seeing Jane. He had a child as well. Priceless.” He tapped the wheel. “Maybe Jane found out the doctor was married and threatened to cause trouble.”

“Let’s see if Jane mentioned this *murder*, to anyone else.” Stacey said, rubbing her thumb over the scar on her right palm.

“Do they bother you?” Brian asked, glancing her way.

He was referring to the deep cuts across both of Stacey’s palms. Injuries she received as part of the Malicourt case when a man now in prison awaiting trial for multiple murders and a list of other disturbing crimes, set up a vicious booby trap.

“Sometimes,” she replied, placing her hands in her lap. “But it’s more numbness than pain. I’m regaining movement, but sometimes it tingles. Maybe it’s my spider sense,” she said with a straight face. “My hands tingle when I hear bullshit.”

Brian laughed. “If that’s the case, listening to the doctor talk must have practically set your hands on fire.”

Chapter Nineteen

Noise from the bar below drifted up in bursts of laughter and sometimes jarring cries. Veronika tossed the bag of items she'd purchased from the mini-mart on the bed. A toothbrush, plastic comb, deodorant and a man's T-shirt: bare essentials for a night in Seabreak. With the exception of her underwear, which she would rinse out in the tiny bathroom, her clothes would have to do for another day. Physically exhausted but mentally wired, she took a shower.

The pressure was sufficient, but the water temperature was barely above tepid. As the spray hit the back of her neck, she closed her eyes and saw Jason Reece hanging from a rope in his workshop. It wasn't the horror of that image that plagued her, but something else. A gnawing feeling that she was missing something, something vital that dangled just out of reach.

Finished with the shower and wearing the cheap T-shirt, she picked up her phone and brought up the photos she'd taken at the scene, hoping the images would jog whatever it was that was firing in the back of her mind. The images were jarring, but nothing jumped out. In the end, she found herself staring at the photograph she'd taken of Jason Reece's driver's licence picture while behind her, the bathroom tap dripped. He was an ordinary-looking man, heavy around the jowls with the ruddy complexion of a heavy drinker.

With no sign of foul play, forensics had taken less than an hour to process the scene. While the team from Joondalup found nothing out of place, Veronika wasn't convinced. The timing of the man's death didn't sit well. It screamed, but just what it screamed, she didn't know.

Richard Wilson knew about the renewed investigation because he had the manager of the storage units in his pocket. Was someone else feeding him information? Was it possible that when Veronika asked him about his wife's visit to Seabreak in 2000, Richard realised they were looking into Adella Reece's disappearance? Did he tell Jason Reece? If so, why? And why would Jason Reece take his own life? Did he have something to hide? But, more importantly, if it wasn't Richard, who leaked the information about the renewed interest in the case?

The questions were piling up, but the answers were still nowhere to be found. One thing was clear, Adella was the key. She had to be the answer to unravelling Jane's disappearance. In all likelihood, Jane was in Seabreak when Adella went missing, and Jane had a clipping about Adella's case hidden in her possessions.

Veronika set her phone down and tucked her still damp hair behind her ear. She was positive that the clipping Jane kept and wrote on meant something.

"Why keep it hidden in a book?" she said aloud.

Suddenly, Veronika had an idea. It was late, almost eight o'clock, but there was something she had to know. She pulled out the inventory of items taken from Jane's storage unit and scanned the list. What she was looking for wasn't there.

Brian answered on the first ring.

"Sorry to call so late," Veronika said, "but do you remember the title of the book you found the clipping in? On the inventory list it just says paperback."

Brian seemed unperturbed by the lateness of the call. "No, sorry, boss, I was too focused on the clipping," he replied. "I have the book in evidence. I can check tomorrow."

She thanked him and then gave him the rundown on what they'd found at Jason Reece's house.

"Holy shit," Brian said. "Why would he suddenly top himself?"

"That's what I'm trying to figure out," she responded. "Jim and I are staying in Seabreak for the time being. I still need to speak to the local police, Jason Reece's friends, and hopefully, Richard's brother. Can you let the team know in the morning? Also, send me a photo of that book."

"Will do. I'll have the picture to you first thing," Brian assured her. "But there's something else. I was going to brief you tomorrow, but I'm thinking it can't wait."

"Go on," she urged.

Brian explained that he and Stacey visited Jane Wilson's psych at his home.

"He said Jane was experiencing a break from reality," Brian continued. "She said she felt guilty because she'd witnessed a murder."

The news took a second to sink in and then Veronika's mind was working, jumping from fact to fact and landing on supposition.

"You there, boss?" Brian asked.

"Yes," she replied absently. "Keep me posted. I'll talk to you tomorrow."

She set the phone down on the bed. Connections were dropping into place at a furious speed. The ticking sensation in Veronika's brain was racing as she pieced together a theory. There were still holes – enormous holes, but if what she was thinking was correct or even close, she was onto something.

* * *

Once dressed, she put in a call to Mandurah Police Station hoping Culla could give her some background on Candice Burns. If there was something that connected her to Adella and Jane, no matter how insignificant, it might be the break in the case they needed. The call was answered by a public servant managing the desk, who told her that Sergeant Culla had taken a few days' leave. Veronika thought about asking for Culla's personal number, but decided her questions could wait a few days. Or at least until they spoke to Candice's parents.

Ending the call, she texted Jim and asked him to meet her in her room. It was 8:30 a.m., late enough to drive to the local police station and expect it to be open, but she wanted complete privacy and a chance to go over the evidence before deciding on her next move.

When she opened her door to Jim, he was carrying two takeaway drinks: coffee for him and tea for her.

"Did you get any sleep?" he asked, setting the drinks down on the nightstand.

"Some," she replied, taking the lid off her tea. "That damn dripping tap kept me awake half the night."

What she really needed was coffee, something sugary, a decent hairdryer and her laptop, but for now, tea would have to do.

"I want to go over the case before we go any further," Veronika began.

Jim sat on the bed and spread his arms wide, indicating for her to continue. She began by relaying what Brian had told her about Jane's psychologist.

"It's safe to say Jane Wilson is dead," she continued. "We know she had problems with anxiety and depression, which, according to her father, began when she was in her teens. Jane visited Seabreak as a teenager and we are fairly certain the visit coincided with Adella Reece's disappearance. We also know Jane had a newspaper clipping detailing Adella's case." Veronika walked to the window, then back to the bed.

"Jane made no secret of the fact that she was nervous about returning to Seabreak," she continued. "She told her psych she had witnessed a murder and then, a few months later, she returns to Seabreak and goes missing herself. We start asking questions about Adella Reece, but before we can interview her husband, he hangs himself." She stopped pacing. "Does all this sound too connected to be a coincidence?" She opened her mouth to continue when Jim interrupted.

"I know. I know you don't believe in coincidences." He ran a finger under his chin. She'd worked with him long enough to know he was thinking, so she gave him time.

"You think Jane saw something when she was in Seabreak as a kid," he said. "Something, maybe a murder, that messed her up. She kept the clipping because she couldn't get past whatever it was she'd witnessed. Then, fifteen years later, Jane's back in Seabreak and?"

Veronika's shoulders slumped. "I don't know. Maybe she recognised the killer, or the killer recognised her."

"Jason Reece?" Jim offered.

"It's a possibility," Veronika said. "But he had an alibi for the night his wife went missing."

"So, we check his alibi," Jim replied. "What about Jane's psychologist? From what you've told me, the man doesn't sound whiter than white."

"Agreed. We're not ruling him out, but first we need to talk to the local police and find out a bit more about Jason Reece."

They were about to leave when Veronika received a text from Brian. An image of a book cover, old and dog-eared: *On the Beach* by Nevil Shute. Veronika stared at the photo and a realisation hit her. The word Jane wrote in the clipping's margin wasn't a name, but a word: Dunes.

Chapter Twenty

"Edward Wilson?" Veronika held up her identification. "I'm Detective Inspector Pope."

There was an echo of his brother's face in the man's features, but a certain strength in the jaw and eyes gave him a tougher outdoorsy handsomeness that Veronica associated with farmers and jackaroos; men who spent their lives in the sun and wind.

"What do you want?" The question was clipped and the man's already strong features hardened as he kept her standing on the doorstep.

"I spoke to your brother yesterday about his wife's case. I'd like very much to speak to you about Jane."

After seeing the book cover, she'd asked Jim to drop her off at Edward Wilson's house and take the lead in dealing with the local police and tracking down Jason Reece's alibi for the night his wife went missing.

"I don't have anything to say to you people. You've done nothing but cause my brother pain." Edward's voice was deeper than his brother's and edged with anger. "I've been working all morning, so the last thing I want–"

"It's not what you think, Mr Wilson. If you'll just give me a few minutes, I'll explain," Veronika insisted. "You don't have to say anything, and if you don't like what I have to say, I'll go." He seemed momentarily undecided, so she pushed on. "There's been some developments in the case. I'd truly like to put things right, if you'll just give me a chance."

"A few minutes," he said, stepping aside and holding the door open.

He led her into the main room and gestured for her to sit at a huge dining table.

"What a view," she said, taking a seat facing the window that dominated most of the room. "I'm sure you never get tired of this."

He grunted and sat opposite her with his back to the ocean. Veronika usually liked to keep her cards close to her chest when working on a case, but if she hoped to get anywhere with Edward, she'd have to be frank. Or as close to it as she could afford to be without compromising the investigation.

"Your brother is aware of our renewed efforts to find his wife," she began. "A lot has changed since the initial investigation and I can assure you that we are looking into Jane's disappearance with an even-handed approach."

He remained stony faced and unmoved. "The new developments?"

"Your sister-in-law's disappearance may have been connected to another case. Something that happened when Jane was a teenager," Veronika said, choosing her words carefully. "It's still early days on the investigation, but it's a line of inquiry that we're keen to follow."

For the first time since she'd met him, Edward's expression relaxed somewhat.

"Do you know a man named Jason Reece?" she asked.

Edward looked down at his hands. "I know of him. Why do you ask?"

"In 2000, his wife went missing. We believe Jane was in Seabreak at the time and may have seen something."

She waited and let the words sink in. Edward continued to stare at his hands.

"In the initial police report, you told Sergeant Culla that your brother mentioned having a strange conversation with his wife the night she disappeared. What was that conversation about?"

"Why don't you ask Richard," he snapped.

"I will, but the following morning, when he discovered his wife was gone, was very traumatic for your brother and he was taken to hospital. Perhaps *your* memory of that day is clearer."

"He said they had a weird conversation," he replied. "She was talking about the past and things that had happened to her."

"Did he give you any specifics?" she asked.

He shook his head. "That's all he told me. I asked if they'd had a fight, thinking she might have stormed off. But Richard said it was just a weird conversation."

While the details were paper thin, what Edward was telling her jelled with her theory that Jane saw something when she was a teenager.

"You said you knew of Jason Reece," she said. "In what capacity?"

"I don't know. It's a small town, you hear names," he said, rising from the table. "I've given you a few minutes. Now I want you to leave. I'm beat and I need to sleep."

Veronika didn't protest, but as he walked her to the door, something occurred to her. Something that had been bothering her since the night before when she was studying the picture of Jason Reece's workshop.

"You're a cray fisherman, aren't you?" she asked, pausing while he held the front door open for her.

"Yeah, why?" Edward looked cautious.

"Is there anywhere in town where you can buy rope?"

* * *

She entered the same mini-mart she'd been in the day before, but at the time, hardly noticed the bait fridge and fishing gear on display. While the shop was only a ten-minute walk, the morning sun was intense and her already crumpled shirt clung to her back like a clammy hand.

"Can you point me towards the rope?" Veronika asked the attendant behind the counter.

"You were in here yesterday," he responded, looking up from an open newspaper. A rake of a man with globular eyes behind thick lenses squinted at her. "You staying at the campground on Tanmoore Street?"

"Campground?" she asked, confused.

"The rope. It gets blowy early morning. Most campers aren't ready for the wind up here," he explained. "You've got to tie close to the ground, but you'll still get the flapping. Nothing stops the tent flapping."

He was wearing a dark blue crew-neck shirt and a name badge that was smeared with something brown. Veronika hoped it was barbeque sauce. The smudge partially obscured the man's name, leaving only *ve* visible.

"Right," she replied. "Is the rope with the fishing gear?"

"No, love, what you want is down there," he said, coming around the counter and pointing to the second aisle.

For a mini-mart, there was an impressive variety of rope; three variations on display. Thick grey rope hung in great coils. She guessed they stocked it for the local fishermen. There was also narrow green cord, the sort used for securing items on the back of trailers and utes. Finally, there were a couple of rolls of black and yellow nylon rope, the sort she supposed that campers favoured. Nothing orange. Nothing like the rope Jason Reece used to hang himself.

"Dave," she said, taking a stab at the man's name. "Do you ever stock orange rope?"

The shopkeeper, back behind the counter and concentrating on his newspaper, glanced up. "No orange rope, we don't stock the cheap stuff, just what's on the shelf." His bulbus eyes were shiny with curiosity. "You don't look like a camper, not in that get-up." He nodded to her black pants, jacket, and shirt. "What did you say you needed orange rope for?"

Veronika produced her badge and identified herself. "Did this man come in here looking for rope?" she asked, showing him Jason Reece's licence photo on her phone.

"So, this *is* about Jason," he replied. "I thought you were a cop. You have that look."

She didn't take the bait and ask what *that* look might be. Instead, she asked, "Do you know him?"

"I know his place was crawling with cops yesterday," Dave said, removing his glasses.

Sloppy name badge aside, Dave seemed fairly switched on. If he knew about the crime scene, she saw no reason to be evasive.

"Who told you that?" she asked.

"No one told," he replied. "I saw it with my own eyes, what's left of them. I live on the same street as Jason. Across the way, sort of diagonally. I saw the cops and an ambulance. Now you're here asking about rope, so I'm guessing I won't be seeing Jason anytime soon."

"That's correct. It appears that Mr Reece took his own life and I'm trying to figure out why," she responded.

"Jesus." Dave picked up his glasses, went to put them on, then stopped. "It doesn't make any sense. He was talking about ordering some parts for the mower he was working on. That's how he made his money, fixing up old mowers and selling them. Lot of people like the old ones and Jason loved tinkering. He got a lot of pleasure out of fixing things.

"We were planning on driving to Perth to take a couple of fixer-uppers to a swap mart next weekend." He bit his lower lip.

She could see he was struggling to keep his emotions in check. "You were friends," she said, softening her voice. "It must be a shock. I'm sorry."

"It's fucking unbelievable. Sorry," Dave said. "It just doesn't sound like him."

"How so?" Veronika asked.

"He was a good bloke," he said, leaning on the counter. "He liked a drink and a bet, but he wasn't depressed. Life threw him some shitty sticks, but he always kept going. To do that; to kill himself. It just doesn't sound like the Jason I know. Knew," he said.

Veronika could see the man was genuinely shaken. She thought of telling him that one never really knows what another person is thinking, that there isn't always an outward sign of a mind in turmoil. While all that was true, she wasn't convinced that Jason Reece had been a man in turmoil. At least not enough to take his own life.

"Did you see anyone at Jason's place the night before last?" she asked.

"I don't see well at night," he replied, tapping a finger to his socket. "Macular degeneration. I'm mostly night-blind, but I did see a set of headlights on my window at around eleven o'clock. I got up from watching television and looked out the front window. There was a car, I saw the lights. But I couldn't make out anything else."

"Coming or going?" she asked.

"Going. The lights dimmed as the car drove away and I saw red taillights."

Veronika thought for a moment. "But you didn't see a car arriving?"

"No." He drew the word out. "I nodded off and didn't wake until around ten, so they might have arrived before then. You think maybe someone brought Jason some bad news?" Dave asked.

There was hope in his eyes. He was seeking reassurance. Some morsel of reason he could grasp onto. If not, she knew Dave would tell himself that he should have seen the signs, he should have done more to help his friend.

"Yes," she replied. "That might have been the case."

There was relief in the man's eyes, but also concern.

"You mentioned Jason being thrown some shitty sticks. What did you mean?" she asked, knowing she was pushing the man; asking probing questions when he was still reeling from the news she'd just delivered.

"His wife. He lost her a long time ago. It was hard on him, the not knowing." He shook his head. "She went missing. They never found out what happened to her."

"Did you know her, Jason's wife?" Veronika asked.

"Not to talk to, apart from hello," he replied. "This was before me and Jason became mates. I saw her around and she'd come into the shop. A good-looking woman, that's for sure." He seemed like he wanted to say more, but stopped.

"And?" she prompted.

"Well, she was a bit flighty. Liked attention." He grimaced with discomfort. "She liked the young blokes. Jason never said, but I reckon he had his hands full there."

Everything Dave told her backed up what Culla had said about Adella Reece. Part of her was starting to believe that Jason Reece might have killed his wife and then years later killed Jane Wilson. If not for the convenient suicide, the theory would be more solid. Maybe he talked about his marital problems with someone else.

"Do you think Jason's wife killed herself?" Veronika asked. "Walked into the ocean?"

"Killed herself," Dave repeated. "Jason didn't talk about her much. But the few times when he mentioned Adella, he said she would have come back to him if she could."

Veronika was still mulling the last part over when Dave continued. "But the cops didn't want to touch the case."

"Why do you say that?" she asked.

He shrugged. "Her reputation, I suppose. Or..." He trailed off, looking sheepish.

"Or what?" she prompted.

"The cops were different back then. A woman like Adella didn't rate much concern. And things were picking up in town. The windsurfers were showing up in summer and business was starting to boom. Missing women are bad for business."

He held up his hands. "I'm not saying it was right, but in a small town, people couldn't risk rocking the boat. Upset the local cops and the next time some drunk smashes your windows, the boys in blue might take a week to turn up and take a report."

It would be easy to dismiss Dave's thoughts on country policing especially back at the turn of the century. But Veronika had seen enough to know that in a place the size of Western Australia, small towns could feel like the wild west.

"Windsurfers," Veronika said, thinking out loud. "Do you get many regulars? People who show up every year?"

"Oh yeah. Fanatics." Dave chuckled. "Who'd have thought the damn wind would be good for business."

"Did Jason have many friends?" she asked, switching gears.

"He lived here all his life. Even did the odd shift here and at the petrol station, so he knew most of the locals. He'd have a drink at the pub. People liked him. But no one close." Dave scratched his chin. "I wish he'd have come over to my place the other night and hashed it out, whatever it was."

Veronika nodded, but if her suspicions were correct, when Jason's guest left, he wasn't in any condition to go anywhere.

"On last thing," she said. "Is there anywhere else in town that sells orange rope?"

Chapter Twenty-one

"Sergeant Margaret Nuse, you heard of her?" Jim asked.

They were eating fish and chips, seated at a plastic table in a park overlooking the water. It was barely past midday, and the temperature was already north of thirty degrees. The sea breeze made the heat tolerable – almost – and buoyed the gulls as they hung and swayed in the air above the table.

"I met her at a strategic planning seminar in Fremantle," Veronika replied. "Serious, but human. From what I remember, she's not a game player."

"She was helpful. Jason Reece was pulled over six years ago for erratic driving, but he passed a breathalyser test. Nothing else of note," Jim continued. "His wife's case is still open, but nothing new since the initial investigation. It's like Culla said, the belief is that Adella drowned, and her body was never recovered."

"Jason's alibi?" Veronika asked.

"I called his mate, the one he was with the night Adella went missing. He's solid. Adamant that Jason was with him. Said a couple of mates could verify that Jason was with them that night," he replied.

"And the Jane Wilson case?" she asked. "Did Margaret have anything to add?"

"Nope," he said. "Before her time and above her pay grade. Her words, not mine."

Veronika wiped her hands on a paper napkin and filled him in on her brief meeting with Edward Wilson and her conversation with Dave at the mini-mart.

"So, Jason had a visitor the night he died," Jim said. "Could change things."

"And," she added, "not everyone in town believed that Adella killed herself."

Veronika pulled out her phone and brought up the photos she took in Jason's workshop.

"There's more," she said. "At first, I couldn't work out what bothered me about these images." She held the phone for Jim to see. "Then when I was talking to Edward Wilson, it hit me. It's the rope. Everything in the workshop is old; used parts, old tools, and then there's this." She pointed to the screen, and the rope strung from the overhead beam and swallowed under the swollen flesh of the dead man's neck.

Jim stared at the image for a second. "It's new," he said, surprised.

"Yes, but then I wondered if Jason went out and bought the rope with suicide in mind. The thing is," she continued, "they don't sell this type of rope in Seabreak. I rang the petrol station and the campground after I spoke to Dave."

"So, if Jason Reece bought the rope, he would have had to drive out of town to find this particular type," Jim said.

"Seems like a lot of effort" – she swiped her phone and brought up another image – "particularly when there is an old rope hanging on a hook in the workshop." She zoomed in on an image that showed a length of grey rope hanging on a hook in Jason's workshop.

"We need to take another look around Reece's house and workshop," Jim said, scrunching up the fish and chip paper.

Veronika was already on her feet. She had been thinking the same thing, but there was something she wanted to see first.

"Give me a minute," she said, tossing her lunch paper in the nearest bin and heading for the beach.

The park ended at a sandy dip with a path through shallow dunes that led to the flat of the beach. Veronika's boots weren't exactly beach wear, and the sand was bone dry and shifting underfoot. Overhead, the gulls circled and squalled, diving towards Jim and Veronika's recently abandoned table in search of scraps.

Once on the beach, the sand was damp and firmer as she made her way towards the shoreline. The ocean was magnificently in motion, alive with a shallow swell, throwing up salt-tinted air as sweet as any she'd tasted. But the view, breathtaking as it was, did nothing to hold her attention.

Turning south and gazing up the beach, Veronika looked not at the water, but at the sand. She stared at the endless expanse of white as it formed peaks, in some places ten metres high. On the ocean, brightly coloured windsurf sails skimmed and bounced over the surface of the water.

"What is it?" Jim asked, jogging towards her, kicking up sand. "What are you looking for?"

"There," she said, pointing north. "Richard and Edward Wilson's house is just before that curve where the land juts out. We are at the far end of town, so these are the dunes. The dunes Jane was recalling when she wrote the word on that newspaper clipping. I'll bet my lunch money that whatever she saw happened somewhere between where we are now and the Wilson house. It happened in those dunes," she said, pointing up the beach as the breeze whipped back her hair.

* * *

As Jim pulled the car into Jason Reece's driveway, Veronika's phone pinged with a reminder. A meeting with Grayson. A full briefing on the case to date. He was already pissed at her for going over his head to the assistant commissioner to get the Wilson case reopened. If she had any chance of keeping the investigation on track, the only way to do so was to show they were making progress.

"Damn," she muttered and checked her watch.

It was almost 1:00 p.m. and the meeting was set for 3:30 p.m. If they left now, she'd make it to the city in time to throw on the clean shirt she kept in her office.

"What's up?" Jim asked, turning off the engine.

She told him about the meeting. "I look like something the cat dragged in."

"We could always come back," he offered, not disagreeing about her rumpled appearance. "Drive back in the morning. That would give us time to speak to Candice Burns's parents."

She knew there were other options: hire a car and drive back to Perth and leave Jim to go over the crime scene. She trusted him. He was an outstanding detective, more than capable of handling a simple job alone. But, if she left, dropped out of this part of the investigation, she risked losing the momentum that was pushing her forward. And, in some ways, she'd be abandoning her responsibility to Jason Reece.

"It is important," he continued.

"So is this," she responded, putting her phone away.

"I can talk to Candice Burns's parents. Vee, you should really–"

"I know, but we'll make it quick," she said, getting out of the car.

She could see he was disappointed, but trying not to show it. Maybe the disappointment was because he knew how important it was to keep Grayson on their side *or* perhaps it was because she didn't trust him enough to leave the search in his hands. Truthfully, she didn't trust anyone's eyes to see the things she saw, to pick up the minor anomalies that could speak louder than words. Why did she believe she was so much more astute than everyone else? Was it a need for control? Could that be the real reason she was struggling with her son's plans to move out and start his own life? Was she worried about losing him or losing control?

"You're right," she said to Jim across the top of the car. "That petrol station we saw on the way in had a car hire sign. Can you drop me off there and then come back here?" Before he could answer, she added, "The light in the workshop was out yesterday. Seems odd, don't you think?"

Chapter Twenty-two

The petrol station was shabbier up close. Veronika glanced over at the two ageing hatchbacks with rental signs on their doors and wondered if she'd been too hasty in her decision to hire a car from a regional outfit. Especially one with a Chilly Willy penguin fridge out front. The place certainly looked sharper when they drove into town. Admittedly, she had been half asleep with her thoughts on Adella and Jane when she glanced at the hire sign.

Once inside the shop, the place only got worse. An antique coffee machine, the sort she remembered seeing at the hospital when she was a kid. A Café Bar, that's what they used to call the tan coloured machines that spat out hot water mixed with powdered coffee.

"Machine's out of service," the attendant said from behind the counter, when he saw her looking at the Café Bar. "Soft drinks only; in the fridge over there."

She followed his gaze to the double-door fridge stacked with cans of fizzy.

"That's okay," she replied. "I'm here to hire a car."

"For town use?" he asked with gruff impatience.

She read his name badge, Lester. He looked to be somewhere south of sixty with wiry grey brows glowering over small eyes.

"I need to drive to the city," she said. "Is that a problem?"

"Not for me, as long as you have ID and a credit card," Lester replied. "But it will cost extra. I have a contact in Belmont. You can drop the car off there."

She sighed inwardly. As it was, she would be cutting it fine. Belmont would take her out of her way and add extra time to the journey.

As she filled out the forms, Veronika wondered if Lester was a prick to all his customers, or was she just the lucky one? Some people just flat out hated cops, and they could usually smell them at twenty paces. Cop haters were often individuals who had previous dealings with police.

With the forms completed, she watched Lester sign the papers. Lester West, she noticed his signature and committed the name to memory, at the same time recalling something from the Jane Wilson file.

"You worked here long?" Veronika asked, staring down at the man's bald pate.

"Long enough," he replied, picking up the papers. "I own this place."

"Do you remember Jane Wilson?" she continued, taking out her ID and credit card.

"What is this?" he demanded. "You want a car or not?"

Lester might have been elderly, but he was a tall man with an imposing attitude. There was something threatening about his stance.

"I'll take the car," she added, hand out, waiting for the keys. "You haven't answered the question."

He snatched the keys off a hook behind the counter, slipped the ring onto his finger and spun the keys, then caught them in the palm of his hand. The movement was sudden and designed to intimidate. All the while, he never took his eyes off her face.

Veronika held her ground, hand out, still waiting. Staring into his small shiny eyes, she had the impression he was thinking. Thinking about who she was and who dropped her off at the petrol station. Perhaps he was weighing up the odds of another customer walking in.

She was thinking too. Thinking about the gun on her belt and the stack of cans behind her and how quickly she could spin around and pitch one at the man's face.

The moment stretched, but she remained still – waiting. Finally, Lester dropped the keys into her hand.

"Don't know her," he finally replied.

Veronika took the keys and stashed them in her back pocket, letting her fingers linger near her gun. Something about the man made her uneasy and experience had taught her not to ignore her instincts.

"The police report says she stopped here with her husband the day she disappeared. Did you see her?"

While she knew the report said Richard Wilson entered the petrol station alone and was served by a young woman, Veronika still wanted to see the man's reaction to the question. And, so far, his behaviour was setting off warning bells.

"Well, I didn't see her," he replied.

A few minutes later, in a car that smelled like mouldy plastic, Veronika let out a long breath and started the engine. She could have backed out and turned onto the road, but instead, she pulled a U-turn and rolled past the shop. Through the window, she could see Lester West was on his phone.

Chapter Twenty-three

Jim promised his wife he'd be home for dinner, told her he loved her, and stashed his phone in his back pocket before opening the workshop door. Being away from Julie overnight didn't sit well. More so since Amelie came along. They had waited a long time for a baby. Sometimes, it felt like the job was eclipsing the very thing he'd wanted most; to be a husband and father. More than that, he felt like a fraud because the job had its claws in him, and he couldn't envision himself doing anything else. He didn't want to do anything else.

With the afternoon sunlight streaming through the grimy windows and casting the cluttered workshop in golden light, it was hard to imagine that only a day ago, there was a dead man hanging from the main beam. If not for the lingering smell, there was almost no trace of the tragedy. Jim planted his hands on his hips and focused on the scene.

The floor, rough concrete and coated with a layer of dust, showed signs of the previous few days' activity. Track marks were clearly visible in the dust, creating two clear lines between the workbench and the area under the beam where Reece hung himself. Jim observed these things from his position near the door.

There were scuff marks, and more signs of activity on the floor around the area where the body was discovered, and then removed. He attributed these disturbances to the paramedics and forensic team.

Before inspecting the room, Jim examined the door. Checking the handle and locking mechanism, he found no sign that the door had been forced. Not that an intact lock meant anything. If Jason Reece was in the workshop, why would he bother locking the door? It made more sense that he would leave it unlocked.

Next, he took a closer look at the workbench. A few tools and what looked like machine parts. He noticed one of the mowers in the far corner was partially dismantled. It seemed, just as the guy at the mini-mart had said, Reece was restoring or fixing a lawnmower.

Turning his attention back to the floor, Jim studied the drag marks left by the stool. Something was off. Drag marks in the dust, but no heel marks. How could that be? Also, the workshop looked to be in use, so why so much dust in the centre of the room? Around the corners, yes, but not between the door, bench and row of mowers. It wasn't a big thing, but often, the crucial elements were in the minor details.

Jim scanned the room until he found what he was looking for. A long-handled dustpan and brush leaning against the wall next to the bench. Taking care not to disturb the tracks, he moved and crouched down so he could examine the pan.

Dust, not much but traces. It got him thinking that someone had gone to a great deal of trouble to make sure there were clear drag marks. Too much trouble. Going to such lengths to set the scene; the stool dragged into position in the centre of the room told the story of a man intent on taking his own life. Only whoever set the scene went too far and covered any sign of footprints in the dust.

If the drag marks were to be believed, there should have been heel marks.

Remembering what Veronika said about the light being out, he held the dustpan up and turned to where the light cast a jagged shaft through the grimy window. Amidst the dust, he saw a glint from what looked like a speck of glass.

Jim took out his phone and snapped a few pictures. Near where he was standing, a stepladder leaned against the wall. He carried it to the centre of the room. A single light dangled from an electrical cord with a grey metal shade. The light dangled almost directly above the beam where Jason Reece's body had hung.

Jim unfolded the ladder and climbed up. From his position under the light shade, he could see the bulb was in place but shattered. It could have happened when Jason was tossing the rope over the beam, but if so, why would he go to the trouble of cleaning up the broken glass? Cleaning it up and disposing of it. Just as Veronika said, it was odd.

He snapped a photo of the broken bulb and put the ladder away. When he was done, he moved his search to the house.

The day before, when they found the body, Jim had been in the house. In the heat of the initial search, he'd concentrated on finding Reece's wallet and checking for obvious signs of a struggle or break-in. Now, he looked with a steadier eye.

Still nothing but a typical old bloke's house; outdated furniture, slightly messy rooms and the fading odour of something soupy in the air. The only surprising thing about Jason Reece's living room was the small TV sitting in the corner and not, as was usual, at the heart of the room.

Not a man to watch television, Jim supposed. No, the workshop was his passion. And why not? There was something deeply satisfying about working with one's hands. Jim felt a sudden flicker of sadness for the dead widower. He led a lonely life, yet the man had continued to try to remain productive. That type of resilience rarely jelled with suicidal tendencies.

As Jim surveyed the room, he noticed a picture frame sitting face down on the coffee table next to a stack of newspapers. He used his sleeve to pick up the frame and turn it over. A much younger Jason, his features lit up with a smile and his arm draped around the shoulders of a beautiful dark-haired woman – Adella. Had he been looking at the long-ago happy moment when he decided to hang himself? Why now?

Adella had been gone for over twenty years. Was the memory still painful? Painful enough to make Reece give up on life? Jim pulled an evidence bag out of his pocket and dropped the photo inside. He then searched the room, examining surfaces until he found a spot on the shelf below the television. A clear rectangle in the dust. A place the photograph once occupied.

Done with the living room, Jim turned his attention to the kitchen. Again, nothing extraordinary; a small dining table and chairs, a rotary phone on the wall and a plate crusted with food scraps in the sink; Reece's last meal? In the fridge, Jim found a steak, a plastic tub of wilted salad, and a couple of cans of beer.

Wanting to know if the man had been drinking on the night he took his own life, Jim lifted the lid on the kitchen bin. A fly buzzed out of the smelly receptacle and skimmed his face. Grimacing, he spotted two empty beer bottles. They were a different brand from the ones in the fridge. Staring at the empties, he began to formulate a theory.

Jason got a call. Not from a stranger, but from someone he knew. They talked. Something about the call got Jason thinking about the past, so he went into the living room and picked up the photo of him and his wife. He sat in the old, grey leather recliner and stared at the image. Sometime later, the caller arrives, and Jason lets him in. It would have to have been a man, because what he did to Reece took strength.

At first, the visitor is friendly, bringing beers and wanting to share a drink. Maybe Jason and the visitor threw back a beer, *or* maybe there were two of them. Jason was no lightweight and lifting or strong-arming him onto that stool could have taken two of them. As they struggled to get Jason into the noose, the light bulb was smashed.

Jim let the lid of the bin drop back into place. It was a theory, but that's all it was. Twenty minutes later, when he'd finished searching the rest of the house, he called Joondalup Forensics Unit and put in a request for a rush on the coroner's autopsy on Jason Reece.

Chapter Twenty-four

The meeting was a bust. They were making progress, but not to her superior's mind. Grayson wanted something to take to the media. He wanted the glory of closing a famous case, a feat others had failed to accomplish. And as an incentive, he dangled the possibility of a larger budget if the Wilson case was closed. Veronika wanted to find Jane and bring her family some peace, but she also had to consider the possibility of an increased budget. Other families who would benefit from the expansion of the Special Crime Squad.

No matter how she looked at it, Grayson wanted results.

"You and me both," she said to herself as she gathered up her laptop and left the office.

"Do you have a minute?" Haru asked, catching her on her way to the lift.

She almost asked him if it could wait until the squad briefing in the morning, but stopped herself. With the budget meeting fiasco, it was difficult enough concentrating on how Jason Reece's apparent suicide fitted into the Jane Wilson disappearance. The last thing she needed was another distraction. Still, she reminded herself, every piece of information, no matter how small, was important.

"It can wait until tomorrow morning," Haru said, probably catching the look on her face.

"No," Veronika said. "Tell me."

He looked unconvinced, but continued. "I've been looking at attacks on women and missing women within our search field."

She waited, resisting the urge to hurry him as he found his way to the point. Haru was a perfect addition to the squad; smart, professional, and systematic in his approach to detective work. However, it was his exacting nature that sometimes hampered his communication skills.

"I think I've found something," he said. "Four years ago, Veeta Seckov reported being attacked as she walked home from the beach in Ledge Point."

He had her full attention now. "Go on," she prompted.

"Well, that's about it," Haru replied. "She screamed, fought off her attacker, and ran. She didn't get a look at the man. With no description of the perpetrator and no witnesses, the investigation stalled."

When Haru mentioned the beach, Veronika's mind immediately jumped to Jane Wilson *and* the word she'd doodled on the article about Adella. *Dunes*.

"Email me the details and be ready to brief the squad in the morning," she said, shifting her laptop bag under her arm and pressing the button to summon the lift. "Then go home and get some rest. Tomorrow, see if you can track Veeta Seckov down."

As the lift doors opened and Veronika stepped in, she stuck out her arm and held the door.

"Good work, Haru," she called to the detective as he was about to turn away.

On the way down to the parking lot, Veronika thought about the woman who had been attacked in Ledge Point, but her mind was fogging over with the need for food and sleep. Maybe a long soak in a hot bath would clear her thoughts. When she climbed behind the wheel, all she could think of was Adella and how she was the key to the entire case. Whatever answers Jason Reece might have had were long gone. But maybe there was another way.

Still sitting in the car, she opened her laptop and pulled up Adella's file. In minutes, she found what she was looking for; a name and address for Adella's older sister.

* * *

It took a driver's license check to find the woman's current address, but the news was good. Not only was Elizabeth Crozier alive and well, but she was now living in a retirement village in Perth.

Veronika checked the time; 5:15 p.m. It would be almost dinner time when she arrived in Wanneroo. A little late for a visit, but surprise calls were her specialty.

When she pulled up in front of Adella's sister's home, Veronika was pleasantly surprised by the neat rows of bungalows. What, she wondered, were the weekly fees for a place like Eden Grove? With its lush lawns and flower beds, the village was a far cry from the windswept dunes of Seabreak. *Dunes*: her thoughts kept returning to that word.

Elizabeth Crozier was a petite brunette with the same dark eyes as her sister. Eyes that widened with surprise when Veronika produced her ID and asked to talk to her about Adella.

"I thought the police gave up on my little sister a long time ago," Elizabeth said, holding the door open for Veronika to enter.

She experienced a moment of trepidation. Not fear exactly, but the faint ghost of it. A feeling left over from an incident a few years earlier. A time when Veronika entered a house belonging to an elderly woman, only to be attacked from behind. The ferocity of that attack left her with a fractured skull and ongoing shoulder pain.

It had taken time, a lot of time for her to come to grips with what happened to her in that old woman's house. For a while, it almost consumed her, but now weeks would go by, and she wouldn't think of the assault, only to be jarred back in time by something as simple as Elizabeth Crozier holding the door open for her.

Elizabeth was watching her, the polite expression on her face starting to slip, so Veronika stepped over the threshold.

"We haven't given up," Veronika replied, following the woman into the spotlessly clean sitting room. "In fact, I'm re-examining the case and hoped you could give me some background information on your sister."

"You want some coffee?" Elizabeth asked, halfway into a floral padded armchair.

Veronika almost said yes. After the long drive back to the city, the blow-out meeting with the Commander, all done wearing two-day-old clothes, coffee was precisely what she needed. But that old familiar wariness told her to keep the old lady where she could see her.

"Thank you, but it's a bit late for me," Veronika said.

Elizabeth nodded and sat back. "You're probably right. If I drink it too late, I'm up half the night." The old woman sighed. "She'd be fifty-two now," she said, gesturing to the sofa. "My sister. Still a comparatively young woman, to my mind, anyway. But I still think of her as she was, young and beautiful. She was stunning, even as a baby.

"I was twelve when Addy was born. I think our parents expected me to be jealous, but I loved her from the minute I saw her. She was such a sweet little girl." She stopped talking and fiddled with a loose piece of thread on the arm of the chair.

"When did you last speak to your sister?" Veronika asked.

"It was a long time ago, but I remember her telling me Jason was worried," she began. "I was still living in Seabreak and, well, he was struggling."

"How so?" Veronika asked.

Elizabeth shrugged. "There's no easy way to say this. My sister was running around on him. Things were getting worse with her drinking and the men." The last part came out along with a tired exhale. "She wasn't always that way. When Addy and Jason got married, she was madly in love. All she wanted was a family, but all that changed after the accident."

Confused, Veronika asked, "Accident?"

"About four years before she disappeared, Jason and Addy were in the city for a weekend getaway. They were at a bar in Fremantle. Jason went to fetch the car while Addy waited on the kerb outside the building." The woman shook her head. "A drunk driver came out of nowhere and hit her. She spent two weeks in the ICU. A brain injury, the doctors said. They told us to prepare for the worst, loss of memory, speech, maybe impaired cognitive functioning. They were wrong. Like a miracle, Addy came back to us, but when she came out of the coma, something dark had attached itself to her."

Veronika wasn't sure what Elizabeth meant by something dark, but she didn't want to interrupt the woman's flow of memories by asking too many questions.

"At first, she seemed fine, like her old self. Then things changed. She'd go for days where she was barely able to function. The black dog, I heard that term somewhere as a way of describing depression." Elizabeth grimaced.

Veronika was familiar with the term, which was said to have originated with Winston Churchill as a way of describing his feelings of melancholy and hopelessness.

"That mutt had its teeth in my sister," Elizabeth went on. "She started drinking, and that's not all. Addy became promiscuous, picking up men – young men. Taking risks. Jason was at his wits' end. He loved her, but she kept slipping further and further away. We tried, Jason and I, but no matter what we did, she would still disappear only to surface days later, sobbing with shame and regret. Sometimes injured."

Veronika didn't want to add to the woman's pain, but she had to ask. "Do you think she killed herself? Or, Jason lashed out and hurt her?"

Elizabeth pinned her with her dark eyes. "Jason is a gentle man. He would have done anything to help her. Addy was often depressed, but never mentioned suicide. She telephoned me shortly before she vanished for good. She said she was afraid. There was a man. He wouldn't leave her alone. She sounded terrified. I told her to go to the police, but Addy laughed. It was a sad, hopeless laugh; I can still remember the sound. She said she was the town joke, and the police would never believe her."

"Did she tell you the man's name?" Veronika asked.

"No." Elizabeth closed her eyes. "I pushed her to tell me, but she refused. Why didn't I push harder?" she asked, her eyes imploring Veronika for an answer.

"After," Veronika said, moving the conversation on, "did you tell the police about the man?"

"I told Jason. He said he passed it on, but nothing ever came of it. I should have done something," the old woman continued. "Taken her away from that dreadful town, but I let her down. We all let her down."

Veronika thought about Sergeant Bob Culla and the way he dismissed Adella's disappearance as a suicide. Elizabeth and Jason did their best, but did the police? Adella was certainly let down, but as far as Veronika could see, not by her family, but by the police.

"Have you been in touch with Jason recently?" Veronika asked, preparing herself for what was to come next, for the grief she was about to heap on the old woman.

"No," Elizabeth replied. "Not for a few years. We sort of lost touch. I send him a Christmas card every year and always get one back. It's funny though, if things had worked out differently, if Adella had gone with Jason to the car that day in Fremantle, I believe she'd still be alive today. She'd be a mother just as she'd always wanted." She gave a sad smile. "How's Jason taking the news that the investigation is being re-examined? I hope it's not too painful for him. I should ring him."

"I'm sorry, Mrs Crozier," Veronika began, "I have some bad news for you."

Chapter Twenty-five

Before heading north through Ledge Point, Jim checked his watch. He'd told Candice Burns's parents to expect him around three o'clock and it was already a quarter past. It looked like he wasn't going to be home in time for dinner, let alone be there for Amelie's bedtime. He thought of calling Julie, even went as far as pulling out his phone, but then stashed it back in his pocket and pulled away from Jason Reece's house.

* * *

Lawrence and Elise Burns's neatly kept bungalow, with its cheerful welcome mat and deftly trimmed rosemary bushes, spoke to the elderly owner's sense of hope. Hope that was clearly evident in Lawrence Burns's voice when Jim spoke to him that morning. Whichever way the investigation went, Jim knew the news wouldn't be good for the elderly couple.

At four o'clock on the dot, the Burns's front door opened before Jim had a chance to knock.

"Lawrence Burns." The man introduced himself with a smile.

Jim shook the man's outstretched hand and was surprised by the strength in his grip.

"Come in," Lawrence invited. "Come through, please. Elise is waiting."

The warmth of the welcome made Jim painfully aware of how little he had to offer Candice's father by way of progress on his daughter's case. While Jim had made it clear when he arranged the meeting that this was a routine call, it was obvious the man had his hopes up.

"As I said on the phone," Jim said, following the man into the house, "this is just a routine review of your daughter's case."

"Here he is," Lawrence announced to the woman seated in the small but cosy sitting room.

Clearly, the couple were eager to discuss their daughter's case, so Jim took a seat opposite the woman and pulled out his notebook.

"Mrs Burns," Jim began, "I won't keep you too long. Just a few routine questions." He winced internally, realising he'd used the word routine twice in thirty seconds.

"Call me Elise," she replied. "And please, take as long as you like."

"We're just thrilled that you're still looking for our girl," Lawrence added, sitting on the arm of his wife's chair.

Before Jim could blurt out the word *routine* for a third time, Lawrence raised his hand.

"We're not expecting miracles and we know Candice won't be coming home in the way we hoped," Lawrence continued. "But anything you can do to find her; anything would be a blessing."

As he spoke, Elise leaned towards her husband so that their bodies were touching. An image jumped into Jim's mind; Julie plopping a toy frog on Amelie's damp head as his little girl giggled and splashed in the bath.

Jim cleared his throat before speaking. "Tell me about your daughter. What was she like?"

Jim listened as the couple talked about a young woman with big plans. Plans to enter university as a mature-aged student and study to become a teacher. A woman with friends and a purpose in life.

"I'm sorry," Jim said. "But I have to ask about your daughter's arrest in 2006. It's important that I know who Candice was involved with."

"It was complete nonsense," Elise replied. "Candice was leaving a friend's house. A nice girl, Maddie. Candice hadn't even been drinking, and some policeman stopped her on the street. He said she was drunk." Elise's voice wavered.

Lawrence put his hand on his wife's arm. A steadying hand.

"They realised it was all a mistake and dropped the charges," Lawrence continued, taking up the story. "Candice was a good girl. She worked hard. Two jobs. She'd do weekdays at the caravan park and then pick up a few shifts at the petrol station in Seabreak on the weekend."

He closed his eyes for a second. "In what spare time she had, our girl was learning how to rescue native birds. Saving little things when they were lost or hurt. She was a good girl, Detective. She deserved better." His voice cracked with emotion.

Jim nodded. He could see the couple were upset by his line of questioning, so he did what he could to put the interview back on track.

"In the days leading up to her disappearance, did anything unusual happen? Did Candice mention anyone hanging around? Did she mention being worried about anything?"

Both Elise and Lawrence shook their heads. "No, there was nothing out of the ordinary," Elise replied.

"Okay," Jim said, bringing the interview to a close. "I have no doubt that your daughter was an exceptional young woman. I'm sorry if this has been upsetting, but I have to ask the difficult questions because everything that happened to Candice leading up to her disappearance is vital. Every person she met. Every encounter she had is relevant to the case."

Before leaving, Jim gave Lawrence his card. "Call me if you remember anything out of the ordinary that might have happened in the months leading up to the night she disappeared. Anyone new she mentioned. Any small thing."

Elise leaned forward and clasped her hands together. "Yes, yes, we will. And we are grateful. Please don't think we're not. It's just so…"

"Painful," Lawrence took up. "We'll do anything to help."

The man's face was weathered, freckled and tanned from years, Jim guessed, tending his garden. In comparison, Elise was pale-faced and delicate-looking. If life had taken a different turn and Candice was still alive, the couple would probably be grandparents now. In a different life, they'd be looking forward to holidays and birthdays spent buying gifts and planning celebrations with their family. Instead, they waited and hoped. Leaning on each other for comfort in what had become, for them, a cold world.

"You have helped," Jim replied, standing. "Candice's case is still open. We're still searching."

As he drove south towards Seabreak, Jim couldn't get Lawrence and Elise out of his mind. While on the surface, the things they had told him didn't add much to the investigation, one thing stood out; Candice spent time in Seabreak.

It was a tenuous link, but a link just the same. Now all he had to do was figure out how that link connected Candice to Adella and Jane. His instincts told him the answer was there somewhere.

Chapter Twenty-six

On his way through Seabreak, Jim stopped by the local police station to let Sergeant Nuse know he'd asked for a rush on the coroner's autopsy. Nuse had given him her number the day before so he could have called, but since the death was on her beat and he was in town, Jim felt it only right that he do the talking in person. He was barely out of the car when he spotted Nuse and a constable heading for a patrol car around the side of the station.

"Got a minute?" Jim called as he approached the pair.

Nuse gestured for the constable to wait in the car and then turned her attention to Jim.

"Let me guess," she said, folding her arms and leaning against the police vehicle. "You've been at Reece's house."

With her hair pinned off her collar in a tight bun and an air of amusement in her voice, she reminded him of Veronika. Although they looked nothing alike, there was something in her demeanour, a quiet confidence that struck him as somehow akin to the woman he worked with.

"I'm on my way out of town," Jim said. "And yes, I've been at Reece's house." He filled her in on the autopsy request.

"So, you're not convinced it was a suicide," she said. "Care to share your reasoning?"

He could have brushed her off and kept the information to himself, but so far, she'd been helpful and if his suspicions about Reece were correct, he'd be seeing more of Margaret Nuse.

Jim told her what he'd found at Reece's place. "Something's off," he finished, and waited for her reaction.

"You could be right, Sergeant Drommel," Nuse said, surprising him with her candour. "You go to interview a man and find him hanging in his workshop. It's too convenient. If something is happening in Seabreak, I'd appreciate being kept in the loop."

"No problem," he replied. "And call me Jim."

"Thanks, Jim," she said, turning and opening the car door. "Have a safe drive back to the city."

"You got a job?" Jim asked out of curiosity.

"Missing woman in Ledge Point," Nuse said. "She hasn't been seen since Tuesday night. Her mother called it in about twenty minutes ago."

Jim's mind raced and again he came back to the word, *coincidence*. The whole reason for his presence in Seabreak was to investigate the disappearance of two women. Another missing woman, especially after all these years, could be dismissed as mere chance, but he didn't think so.

"Sergeant Nuse," Jim said, gripping the patrol car's open window. "Mind if I come along?"

Nuse didn't answer right away. Instead, she fixed him with a searching stare. "Hop in," she said, "and call me Madge."

* * *

Once the three of them were gathered outside The Point – the only pub in the small community of Ledge Point – Madge said, "Ashley Simcock's mother rang around after her daughter's boss called on Wednesday to say Ashley didn't show up for her shift at the fish and chip shop. The mother spoke to a girl friend of Ashley's who said she saw her arguing with a man named Evan Malacci at around 11:30 on Tuesday night."

Madge checked her watch. "It's nearly five o'clock, so the regulars will be gathering inside. I'll speak to the bar staff and then we'll head over to Evan Malacci's place."

Jim would have started with Evan and then visited the pub, but this was Madge's show and, for now, he was just a spectator.

"Colin," she spoke to the young constable with shaved sideburns. "Take notes and keep your eyes on the punters. If anyone looks nervous, don't let them out of your sight."

"I'll stay out here," Jim put in, "and take a look around."

Madge fixed him with another of her searching looks. "Right. With any luck, the boyfriend will be at the bottom of this, and we'll wrap it up by nightfall."

She was probably right about the boyfriend. More often than not, that's the way these things played out. The man who claims to be in love with a woman is usually the one who kills her. Or, at the very least, puts her in the hospital. But Jim wasn't convinced this case would be that tragically simple.

Once Madge and Colin entered the pub, he took his time looking over the building's exterior. No visible cameras. There was a parking lot, dotted with utes and a few hatchbacks. Turning away from the entrance, he took up a position near the road and watched as another car pulled in and two men wearing navy overalls and hi-vis vests entered the establishment.

Even with the occasional blast of music and voices as the bar door opened, then swung shut, he could hear the ocean and the crashing waves. Another beachside disappearance. What were the chances?

Leaving the parking lot, Jim walked towards the road that headed north. A couple of vehicles passed by, heading for The Point. Not a busy road, even at peak hour. If the missing woman walked this way at almost midnight, there was little chance that anyone saw her.

A lonely stretch of road with parkland on the right and sand dunes and salt bushes on the left. It all seemed alarmingly familiar. Or was he making connections based on nothing more than the victim's gender and proximity to a beach? A young woman disappears near a beach. An argument with her boyfriend that got out of hand? Did Ashley simply argue with Evan, then take off somewhere to lick her wounds? Or was there something far-reaching and sinister at play?

Jim turned, intending to walk back to the pub, when something grabbed his attention. The sinking sun winked off something metallic on the sand. On closer inspection, he realised the object was an earring. A small silver heart.

Instead of picking up the piece of jewellery, he pulled one of his cards out of his pocket, folded it and placed it in the sand next to the heart. Crouching, he took out his phone and snapped a couple of pictures. From his position close to the ground, he noticed a snapped branch on the bush overhanging the earring and flattened ground a metre or so further towards the dunes. Satisfied that he had what he needed, Jim tried to make a call, only to find that there was no reception.

He headed back towards the pub, pausing every metre until the little arc of bars reappeared on his phone.

"I found something," he said when Madge answered his call.

Five minutes later, Sergeant Nuse came strutting along the path with Colin at her side. Jim showed them the earring, and the flattened ground.

"It looks like someone was pulled into these bushes," he said, pointing at the broken branch. "There are shoe prints going back towards the beach."

He could see Madge taking her time, thinking, processing the likelihood of the earring and the marks in the sand being connected to Ashley Simcock's disappearance. His own thoughts had followed a similar path. A path that led to the balance of probability, where even the slimmest chance was enough.

"Colin," Madge said to the constable. "Stay here and don't take your eyes off this." She pointed to the earring. "Don't touch anything."

To Jim she said, "Let's do this fast. Evan Malacci is in the pub, but I haven't spoken to him yet. And, if the sea breeze picks up and is strong enough, all this" – she pointed to the sand – "will be gone."

When they reached the squad car, Madge popped the boot so Jim could grab the crime scene tape, stakes, markers, evidence bags, and camera.

"Send me the photo of the earring, the one on your phone," she said. "I'll speak to Evan."

Jim did as she asked, not bothering to question her about how she knew he'd already photographed what he found. He was beginning to suspect that Margaret Nuse was wasted on country policing. Once he was ready, Jim jogged back to what he was increasingly sure was a crime scene.

Colin helped him to tape off a six-by-six metre square, starting at the path and going back through the bushes and towards the beach. Once the markers were set up, he re-photographed the scene.

Not wanting to step on the flattened sand or possible footprints, he walked the outside of the tape taking photos of any areas that looked to be disturbed. If he was correct about the earring belonging to the missing woman, forensics would do a thorough search and process the area. What Jim was doing now would be an important step in the initial findings.

Jim and Colin were just finishing up when Madge arrived in the squad car.

"Evan Malacci confirmed the earring looked like one of a set he gave Ashley last week," she said, climbing out of the car. "I spoke to one of his friends who said Evan followed Ashley out of the pub but returned a few minutes later and drank himself unconscious. One of the bar staff confirmed that Evan was still at the pub at closing time. His friend drove him home and said he practically had to carry Evan into his house." She nodded at the taped area. "I've called forensics."

"What are you thinking?" Jim asked.

"I think we've got a situation on our hands," she replied as wisps of brown hair, pulled free from her bun by the growing wind, whipped around her head.

Colin, who had his uniform cap off and was wiping his brow on his forearm, said, "I can wait for forensics."

"Okay," Madge said, more to herself than the constable. Then to Jim, she said, "I'll drive you back to your car and we'll take it from here."

He knew what he was about to say might piss her off, but there was no way around it.

"I'll check with DI Pope and see if she wants me to take the lead on this."

"Right." Madge's stare was steely and her response non-committal. "You think this is the work of the same guy as with your two missing women?" she asked. "The same guy operating for over twenty years?"

"It's a possibility," Jim replied, understating his growing feeling of certainty. "And if it is him, this is the first time he's left any physical evidence behind."

Chapter Twenty-seven

Veronika was on her way home when Jim called. Instead of putting her phone in the holder on the dashboard, she'd tossed it on the passenger seat, which meant she had to pull over to answer.

"Where are you?" she asked before he could begin.

Jim filled her in on the missing woman in Ledge Point and what he'd found at Jason Reece's house.

"Send me a copy of that photo you took from Reece's house." She thought for a second, then continued. "Are you good to stay another twenty-four hours in Seabreak and keep on top of the missing woman, um…" Veronika searched for the name he'd just mentioned.

"Ashley Simcock," Jim said. "Julie won't be thrilled about me spending another night away from home, but she'll be okay. And I'd like to stick with it and see if there is a connection to our case. It's early days, but my gut tells me Ashley's one of ours."

"Anything on Candice Burns?" she asked.

"She came from a nice home. Loving parents." He sounded tired. "Apparently, she spent a bit of time in Seabreak. It could be a link."

Veronika took a moment to digest what Jim had said and then passed on what Haru had discovered about the woman attacked from behind near the beach in Ledge Point.

"Check with the local police and see what you can find out," she said. "It could have just been some creep. I'll have Haru track her down. She might still be living locally. And one more thing," she said before hanging up, "I spoke to Adella's sister. She said there was a man that wouldn't leave Adella alone. A man that scared her."

* * *

"Cannoli," Veronika said, setting the box on the table in the squad room.

Since the Malicourt case, when she first discovered her love of the Italian dessert, she made a point of bringing a box for the team once a week. And, as she'd been up since five o'clock, there was plenty of time to stop at a bakery on her way to work.

"Anchors?" Stacey asked.

"Too early," Veronika replied. "I stopped at that bakery on Murray Street."

It was nine o'clock and the team, minus Jim, were together for a briefing. Veronika began by covering old ground; going over what they knew about Jane and Adella.

"Where are we on confirming the dates on Jane and her parents' holiday in Seabreak?" she asked Stacey.

"Jane's mother remembered calling the police and complaining about a noisy party next door to where they were staying while they were on holiday. Police attended and spoke to Mrs Campion, so I'll follow up today and see if the Seabreak cops have a record of the complaint," Stacey replied, brushing crumbs off her shirt.

"Go through Jim," Veronika instructed. "He's working with the locals, so he's your best point of contact."

Veronika continued the briefing from the head of the room, filling them in on Jason Reece's apparent suicide and her meeting with Elizabeth Crozier.

"The sister confirmed that there was a man hanging around. A man Adella was afraid of." Veronika turned to the board behind her and looked at Adella's photograph. "There is nothing in Adella's file about a man hanging around her. Yet Elizabeth Crozier told Jason to pass the information on to the police."

"Looks like the local cops were set on calling it a suicide and shelving the case," Brian said.

Veronika agreed. "We have two women whose lives intersected. Adella was afraid, and so was Jane. She told her psychologist that she witnessed a murder.

"Then there's Candice Burns; the woman was last seen in Ledge Point in 2007. According to Candice's parents, she spent quite a bit of time in Seabreak. Now, Ashley Simcock, last seen on Tuesday night leaving the pub in Ledge Point." She waited a moment and let the new information sink in. She could see by their faces, they were thinking, weighing up the possibility of the missing women being connected to the Jane Wilson case.

"Haru?" Veronika indicated for Haru to step up and contribute to the briefing.

Haru stood and repeated what he'd told Veronika the previous evening. To her surprise, he seemed less tentative and somewhat more concise in his choice of words.

"I found an address and phone number for Veeta Seckov; she's living in Yanchep."

"The area we're talking about, where these women went missing," Veronika said when Haru sat, "is large but the population is small. Small enough to make four women disappearing unusual. However, we are looking at a substantial timeline; over twenty years. These other missing women, Candice Burns and Ashley Simcock, may be unrelated, but for now, we're not ruling out a connection." She looked around the room. "Thoughts?"

"You think someone got to Reece and killed him to stop him talking to us?" Stacey asked. "Someone who knew we were reopening the Wilson case?"

"Either that, or I need to rethink my stance on coincidences," Veronika replied. "There's a short list of people who knew what we were doing prior to Jason Reece's death; Jane's parents, Richard Wilson and his solicitor, Bob Culla, Jane's friend Caitlin, as well as Richard's contact at the storage unit, and Dr Albian Sharm."

"Sharm's a snake," Brian interjected. "He was hung up on Jane. I think he still is."

Veronika wondered if Brian's interest in the doctor was becoming too personal.

"It might be worthwhile taking another run at him," Veronika replied. "But tread carefully."

They both knew she was talking about the risk of a harassment complaint and the last thing they needed was another lawsuit associated with the Jane Wilson case.

She turned to Stacey. "Take Haru with you and talk to Veeta Seckov, see if she remembers anything that could help us identify the man who attacked her."

When the meeting broke up, Veronika stopped by Brian's desk and noticed a box of evidence from the storage unit on the floor next to his chair.

"Find anything in there?" she asked, gesturing to the box.

"No." He picked up the box and placed it on his desk. "I've been over every item a dozen times, hoping the answers will jump out, but nothing. I'll take it to the evidence room today."

She was about to agree when a thought occurred to her.

"Is the book in there? *On the Beach*?" she asked.

Brian nodded and fished out the sealed evidence bag containing the book. "I've gone over every page hoping she made a note or highlighted something. It's dog-eared but unmarked."

She took the bag. "I'll take this down to evidence myself later," she said and headed for her office.

Sitting at her desk, staring at the book when she should have been typing up her report on Jason Reece, she wasn't sure what she expected to find. The cover, two people on a sandy beach, a blonde man and a slim-figured woman drawn in shades of yellows, blues and reds, looked to be an original print. Did Jane seek this book out because of the title? Veronika had the image on her phone, but looking at the book made the artwork seem more tangible. There was something about the cover that spoke to her, but she couldn't quite grasp what it was saying.

Pulling out her phone, she brought up the photo Jim sent, the one he found on Jason Reece's coffee table. A young couple smiling for the camera. This was a very different Adella, head resting on Jason's shoulder, her eyes crinkled with laughter. The picture was taken outdoors with the couple sitting on a patch of grass afront a wrought-iron fence. Veronika looked from the photograph to the book cover, hoping something would click.

Experience had taught her not to chase the thought. Better to let the idea marinate and hope it would come to her. Something happened on that beach in Seabreak, and while the book might not have the answers she needed, Veronika had a good idea who would. But first, she had another stop to make.

* * *

Veronika knew David Bender from her days in Fremantle, back when she was a senior constable and he was a junior detective. She'd never liked the man's overconfident bravado or his one-sided view of the world.

Parked outside Bender's house, watching him roll a lawn mower onto a trailer, she couldn't help feeling pity for the former detective. Or maybe, she thought, she should envy him because he was out, living an uncomplicated life. The bigger burdens were no longer his to carry. The thought surprised her because it was the first time she'd thought of her job as a burden.

"David," she said, crossing the road and approaching the trailer. "Got a minute?"

He turned and stepped off the trailer, wiping his hands on his khaki pants.

In some ways, he'd aged since she knew him. His hair, always thin, was now shaved close to the scalp. However, once overweight, physical labour had turned fat into muscle, giving him a trim, athletic physique.

"It's been a long time, Pope," he said, hands on hips. "I hear you've climbed your way up the ranks. Good for you," he said with a touch of sarcasm.

"How have you been?" she asked, ignoring his crack about climbing the ranks.

"As you can see," he said, spreading his arms to take in the trailer loaded with gardening equipment, "I'm king of the world."

His sarcasm continued, although she got the feeling he was embarrassed. He wanted to point out how far he'd fallen and beat her to the punchline and, in his own way, save face. But Bender was wrong. She wasn't there to rub his nose in his dramatic fall from grace or to point out how he'd screwed up his last big case. She wanted insight on Richard Wilson. And if she had to put up with Bender's shit to get what she wanted, so be it.

"Well," she said, "you look ten years younger." A bit of an exaggeration, but she was genuinely pleased to see that the former detective appeared to be thriving physically if not emotionally.

"Okay, well, I'm busy, so let's get to it," he said. "What do you want?"

His reaction wasn't a surprise. With a man like Bender, there was no point dancing around the issue.

"I'm working the Jane Wilson case."

He whistled. "You tired of your job, Pope? Because touching that case will put you on the fast track to unemployment."

He was baiting her, trying to get a reaction, but she sure as hell wasn't going to give him one. "Richard Wilson," Veronika said. "Tell me about him."

"What's to tell?" He shrugged. "He got away with murder *and*, as a bonus, he got a payout from the department. Me, I got the shitty end of the stick."

She could have pointed out the obvious and reminded him he went too far when he spoke at a press conference and identified Richard Wilson as a person of interest.

"I just want to know why you were so sure?" she asked.

"What difference does it make?" he said, letting the bravado slip. "Who cares what I think?"

"I care," Veronika said.

Bender was a lot of things, but he was also an experienced detective. She'd taken a leap of faith on the Wilson case, so she knew Bender must have had his reasons for going so far that he lost his job.

Bender frowned and scratched his forehead. "Isn't it obvious? You've read the file. You're the big-time inspector, cracking all the tough cases."

The temperature was already climbing. With the sun beating down on the back of her neck, the last thing she wanted was to go back and forth with a man who was clearly bitter and looking for someone to blame.

"I read the file," Veronika replied, "but I'd like to hear it from you." When he didn't reply, she pushed on. "Look, I'm not asking for every detail. I just want to know what made you stick your neck out on this one."

"Okay," he said, holding up his hands. "The wife was loaded. Wilson rushed her into marriage and within two months, she was gone, which meant he hit the jackpot."

"And?" she pushed.

"And," Bender said, sounding frustrated by the question, "no one in Seabreak ever saw the wife. Wilson turns up with a cracked windscreen. A bloody windscreen and claims that his wife disappeared off the back porch. Come on."

"The seagull–"

"Yeah, the seagull." He gave a scoffing laugh. "Very convenient. When I spoke to him and his brother, they were both guarded. Those two were in on it together, right from the start. If the wife really went missing, he would have wanted to talk, but he shut up as tight as a duck's ass.

"I might be a washed-up cop," he said, his tone growing more passionate. "But I know when someone's hiding something." He jabbed a finger in Veronika's direction. "Richard Wilson was holding out. Heart attack aside, something was off."

"What did Bob Culla say about his initial interview with Wilson?" she asked, knowing the two men would have discussed Wilson in a way that wasn't included in the report.

"He said Wilson was as guilty as sin," Bender replied, turning and closing the back of his trailer.

She was about to thank him for his time when he turned back.

"If you go anywhere near Wilson, be careful. He's not what he seems."

* * *

The building looked even more impressive in the clear morning light. She was taking a risk coming back unannounced, but if she called ahead, Richard Wilson would either refuse to see her or have his solicitor there as his go-between. The only chance she had of getting some genuine answers was a surprise call. Last time they met, Richard struck her as a very polite man, hopefully too polite to slam the door in her face.

"Inspector Pope." Wilson looked surprised, but so far, there was no sign of anger. No reaching for the phone to call his solicitor.

"Call me Veronika," she said. "Could I come in? I want to update you on our progress."

He hesitated, but as she'd hoped, his upbringing got the best of him. "Yes, of course, come in."

"This view," she said when he led her through to the kitchen, "it makes everything seem small. It reminds me of the one in your brother's house."

"Would you like something to drink?" he offered, ignoring her comment on the view.

"Thank you, no." She gestured to the kitchen table and chairs. "I'd like to get down to business."

"Please, sit," he said, taking a chair with his back to the window, just as his twin had done, with the ocean view.

"You said something about recent developments?" he was wearing a black towelling robe over grey track pants and a white shirt. Behind him, the summer sun shimmered off the Swan River while inside the apartment, the temperature was chilly.

"I was in Seabreak yesterday," she began. "But I'm sure you already knew that." She was referring to her conversation with Richard's twin brother. She had no doubt Edward had already filled his brother in on every word they exchanged.

When Richard made no reply, she continued. "I was there to see a man named Jason Reece."

She noticed Richard's left eyebrow twitch. He was surprised or perhaps startled. She couldn't tell which, but he was trying very hard not to show it.

"He took his own life before I could speak to him," Veronika added.

This time, he reacted. "Oh God. I mean what… That's awful."

"It's like he knew we were coming," she continued. "So, I asked myself who would know we were reopening your wife's case and then pass that information on to someone in Seabreak?"

She left the comment dangling, waiting for his reaction. Then added, "You asked to speak to me on Tuesday. A strange request considering you haven't spoken to the police in six years. If you hadn't requested my presence, I would have been in Seabreak interviewing Jason Reece."

"What are you getting at? You think I'm connected to a suicide now? You can't believe I deliberately kept you away from Seabreak so I could have someone kill themselves? How would I even know you were going to speak to Jason Reece that day?" He rolled his eyes. "Do you people really think I'm to blame for everything that happens in that damn town?"

"I would have thought," Veronika replied, "that the logical question would be, who is Jason Reece and what does he have to do with your wife? Or do you already know the answer?"

His expression changed from what looked like exasperated to dumfounded. Whatever else Richard Wilson was, he wasn't skilled at controlling his reactions.

"Well, I sort of know who he is. It's a small town." All trace of indignation had left his voice. "I know the name. But what does he have to do with–"

"Jane?" she finished for him. "I was hoping you could tell me. You see, his wife, Adella Reece, went missing in 2000 and I think your wife knew something about what happened to her, *and* I believe whatever she knew got Jane killed."

Richard took off his glasses and dropped them on the table with the slow, deliberate movements of someone who was exhausted. Veronika had seen this type of defeated reaction before and knew if she applied more pressure, Richard would likely crack. And, when people crack, they are unpredictable.

"Jane was in Seabreak in 2000. She was a teenager. Something happened during that visit that changed her. She told her psychologist she'd witnessed a murder.

"In your initial statement to the police, you said that you had a strange conversation with Jane the night before she went missing. What did she tell you?"

As she spoke, he rubbed the heels of his hands into his eyes like a man coming out of a deep sleep. When he looked up, there were deep creases beneath his eyes; dark circles that spoke of sleepless nights.

"What did she tell you?" Veronika repeated the question.

"Do you really believe that's what got her killed?" he asked, pain clearly evident in his voice.

"I have to know what she told you," she replied, softening her tone. "It's the only way I can find her and end all this. *You* can help me find her, but I need to know everything."

When he finally answered, he was looking down at the table. "Jane was jumpy. I'd never seen her like that. She said–" he hesitated "–she told me that when she was a kid, her family spent some time in Seabreak. A holiday. She'd been to a party, drank too much and wandered onto the beach and into the dunes."

When he said the word dunes, Veronika felt the skin on her forearms prickle.

"There were voices, arguing." His voice sounded dry, as if the words were sticking in his throat. "Sometime later, she crawled out of the dunes and saw a woman. A half-naked woman being attacked. Jane was sure she'd witnessed a murder."

Richard was a smart man. He had to know he was admitting to withholding information, but he seemed past caring.

"She believed the killer saw her and came after her. Oh God, she said he hunted her through the dunes. My poor Jane, she hid for hours." He opened his hands and held them out to Veronika. "She poured her heart out to me, her darkest hours and deepest fears. And I…" He closed his eyes. "Sorry," he groaned and left the table.

He went to the kitchen and turned on the tap. Veronika swivelled in her seat, never taking her eyes off him as he downed a glass of water. When he returned to the table, he slumped into his seat, mumbling another apology.

"I dismissed her," he continued. "I told her whatever she thought she saw was just the mixed-up memories of a drunk kid. I marginalised her fears. In the morning, Jane was gone."

Veronika thought for a moment, digesting everything he'd said. It all added up with what they knew about Jane and her belief that she'd witnessed a murder. Now, Richard had given her confirmation on the where and when that murder supposedly took place, but something was wrong with his story.

"Why didn't you–" she stopped. Things were clicking into place and at least part of the picture was forming in her mind.

She remained still and focused on the man across the table, except for her hand, which she dropped into her lap. Using her thumb, she flicked her jacket back, allowing easier access to her gun. Her mind went back to Bender's warning: *Be careful, he's not what he seems.*

"Why didn't you tell the police?" he finished the question for her. As he spoke, she noticed he was rubbing the inside of his left wrist with his right index finger. Self-soothing. "Isn't that what you were going to ask?"

"Do you mind if I record this?" Veronika asked, leaving the gun and reaching for her phone.

"No."

The force of the word startled her, but she kept her expression neutral. "All right," she replied. "Why *didn't* you tell anyone?"

"Because," he said, picking up his glasses and putting them on, "it was me Jane saw on the beach that night."

Chapter Twenty-eight

It was Friday morning, later than he would have liked, but sleep hadn't come easy. Jim remembered checking his watch at a little after three o'clock in the morning. From there, he'd fallen into a restless slumber only to wake up at 8:50 a.m. with the inside of his mouth tasting like ground mealworms.

Sitting on the edge of the bed, he could hear the ocean over the sounds of glasses clinking and doors slamming. Sleeping above a bar wasn't his idea of a holiday, but with any luck, he would be back in Perth by nightfall. On his way to the bathroom to take a shower, he tried Evan Malacci on the number he'd given Madge the day before.

"Of course," Jim muttered when Malacci didn't answer.

He'd only spoken to the young man for a few minutes the day before, but had the impression he wasn't the brightest spark. Still, in the cold light of day, he might be able to provide Jim with a few useful answers.

Twenty minutes later, Jim put on his sunglasses and climbed behind the wheel. He thought of stopping by the address Malacci provided, but had a hunch where he'd be more likely to find him. When he pulled into The Point's parking lot, he wasn't surprised to see the squad car parked near the entrance. When Madge dropped him back at his car the previous evening, she said she wanted to re-interview the bar staff and take another look around. It looked like she had got off to an early start.

"Rough night?" Madge asked when Jim stopped at the bar where she'd been engaged in conversation with the bartender.

He ordered a glass of orange juice and downed it in a few gulps. "The beds in that place in Seabreak feel like they're made of limestone blocks," he said.

"There's a cot in the back of the station," she offered. "If you're planning on hanging around, you're welcome to it."

He didn't relish the thought of another night away from home or the idea of sleeping at the Seabreak Police Station, but it was a decent offer. One she didn't have to make, especially as he was stepping on her toes with his continued involvement in the Ashley Simcock case.

"Thanks," he said. "I might have to take you up on that. But not tonight. Depending on what I get out of him," Jim said, gesturing to where Evan Malacci was hunched over a drink in the corner, "I'll drive back to Perth and grab a change of clothes. Plus, I've got another case on the go."

"I don't think you'll get much out of him in that state," Madge muttered and turned back to the bartender. To the bartender, she said, "Time to cut him off."

Jim could tell by the man's glassy eyes and flushed cheeks that the drink he was nursing wasn't his first drink of the day.

"Did you find her?" Evan asked when Jim approached. His unfocused eyes jumped from Jim's face to a point over his right shoulder. He had an empty shot glass in front of him and his hand around a bottle of beer.

Jim shook his head and sat opposite the man. "We're working on it," he said. "When Ashley left you at the pub the other night, did you notice anyone hanging around? Any cars pulling out of the parking lot?"

"You think I would have let her go off on her own if…" He was slurring his words. "If there was something like that."

Jim was beginning to think Madge was correct, and he was wasting his time.

"Did Ashley mention anyone hanging around? Another man she was seeing?" Jim asked.

He didn't see Malacci swing.

Jim heard Madge yell, "Oi."

There was a popping sensation in Jim's head when the bottle Evan was holding exploded against his temple. A spot of light, like the after burn of the sun, blurred Jim's vision. Something shifted under his hands before a blinding pain sliced through the other side of his head. As the lights dimmed, he heard a woman's voice calling his name, and he thought of Julie.

Chapter Twenty-nine

After her third attempt, Stacey gave up trying to reach Jim and put in a call to Seabreak Police Station.

"Oh yeah," Constable Colin Wexler said when she identified herself and explained what she needed. "We've got one of your guys up here helping with a missing woman."

Stacey heard papers rustling. "It's pretty busy, but I'll take a look at our records," Wexler continued. "I think the details would have been logged in the old incident book. What year did you say?"

Stacey resisted the urge to tut and repeated the year, month and name of the complainant.

"Can you get the information to me ASAP?" she asked. "We need to confirm a timeline in a very sensitive case."

Constable Wexler took her number and assured her he'd get back to her before lunch. Judging by his laid-back attitude, she had a feeling she'd be waiting way past lunchtime for a call back.

"And if you see DS Drommel," she said, before hanging up, "can you ask him to call me?"

* * *

Veeta Seckov agreed to meet them at a café in the same shopping centre where she worked as a supermarket cashier. A small woman with brassy hair and angular features, she strode into the coffee shop, surveyed the patrons, and walked directly over to the table where Stacey and Haru were waiting.

"You cops," she said, more as a statement than a question.

Momentarily taken aback by the woman's directness, Stacey introduced both herself and Haru.

"I have fifteen minutes," Veeta said, taking a seat. "Black coffee, three sugar."

"Haru," Stacey gave the detective constable an apologetic look.

"You are boss?" Veeta asked Stacey when Haru left the table and went to the counter to get the woman's coffee.

"Something like that," Stacey replied.

"You tell him jump," Veeta observed, "he jumps."

"Thank you for meeting us," Stacey said, bringing the conversation back on track. "I know it's a difficult thing to talk about, so I'll make this as brief as possible."

"*You* know this?" Veeta asked with a note of defiance.

"I know what it is like to be attacked," Stacey replied.

Veeta narrowed her gaze and her eyes, like blue ice chips, didn't waver.

Stacey held the woman's stare. Over the course of her career, Stacey had been punched, spat on and had her hands sliced open by a home-made booby trap. Still, she wasn't sure any of that measured up to the terror of being grabbed off the street as a civilian.

Veeta gave a slight nod, as if satisfied with whatever she saw in Stacey's eyes. "It was late," she began. "We left the beach and my friend drove away. I walk. I prefer walk, good for the heart."

Haru returned with the coffee and set it down in front of the woman.

"Three sugar?" she asked, eyeing him with suspicion.

"Three," Haru confirmed and took his seat.

"I hear noise behind," Veeta continued. "When I look, nothing. I walk and he grabbed me like this." She put one hand over her mouth and the other across her chest. "He lift me back to the bushes." She took a sip of coffee.

"I think Australia is a safe place for me, but I was wrong," she continued. "He was strong, I think, big. I fight. Kick, use my arms." She made an elbowing gesture. "I make myself small, then run."

"You slipped through his grasp," Stacey offered.

"Yes," Veeta agreed. "I slip and run. I scream and keep running."

The way she told her story, the unemotional recount, together with the unflinching defiance in her eyes, made the words powerful in their rawness. Stacey couldn't help feeling in awe of the woman's stoicism.

"Did he say anything?" Stacey asked. "When he grabbed you?"

"He called me slut," she replied, and for the first time, there was emotion in her voice.

"He say, slut, you always do this," she said the words with disgust.

"I'm sorry," Stacey said. "What he said, what he tried to do, I'm sorry that happened to you." Her hands were clasped together on the table. When she spoke, she opened them, palms out.

Stacey wasn't sure why she did it; expose her scars in that way. Part of her wanted Veeta to know that she meant what she said, that her words weren't just platitudes. But more than that, Stacey wanted the woman to know she understood the determination it took to stay strong under the weight of fear.

Veeta glanced at Stacey's hands, and just for a second, her eyes softened.

"Can you recall anything about him?" Stacey prodded. "His accent? Did he sound young or old?"

"Australian. Not young, but strong," she replied. "I tell the police all this and nothing." She picked up her coffee and drained the cup. "Now you ask the same questions. I thought Australia was a safe place for me, but now I look over my shoulder." She pushed back her chair. "Come see me when you catch him," Veeta said, and left the café without another word.

Chapter Thirty

The air in the apartment was too cool, making Veronika want to shiver. Richard's words hung in that air, threatening to change the temperature between them. Hand in her lap, she was aware of the fabric of her work pants, the texture under her fingers. Sounds seemed sharper. The sunlight felt brighter. Whatever she did next could mean the difference between closing the case or putting herself in harm's way.

"Are you telling me," she said, "that you killed Adella?"

Before he could answer, her phone vibrated. The sudden shock made her hand jump in her lap.

"No," he replied. "No, no. I'm telling you I was with her that night." Perhaps seeing disbelief in her eyes, he persisted. "I swear she was alive when I left her."

Still hyperalert, she felt her hands relax ever so slightly. "Tell me," she said, taking out her notebook and placing it on the table, "everything."

When he saw the notebook, his eyes widened. He was on the verge of something, a disclosure that could blow the case wide open. Given his history with the police, the last thing she wanted to do was spook him. She was also aware that she was alone with him and had let no one know where she was.

"I just need to be clear on the details," she said. "That's all."

He was back to rubbing his wrist, but seemed satisfied. "I was home from uni for the summer break, working on the boat with my father and Ed. I'd seen Adella around. She was stunning. Sexy and sad at the same time. She had this dark hair that fell across her face when she tossed her head." He stopped and pushed his glasses up onto the bridge of his nose.

"I was outside the pub, smoking, bored shitless with the same old faces, when she approached me. Sounds like a scene from a bad movie, but she was magic, or at least it felt that way to a geek like me. I was twenty-one at the time and Adella was the most exotic woman I'd ever met."

He waited, wanting her to say something. To tell him she understood, or that he was just a kid. Instead, she let the silence stretch, hoping he'd feel the need to fill it.

"I knew she was married," he blurted out. "People talked. I heard the things they said about her. I knew it was wrong, but I just didn't care." He got up from the table and went to the kitchen.

Veronika watched him fill two glasses with water. He raised one to his mouth and changed his mind and dumped the water in the sink.

"I need something stronger," he muttered, opening the cabinet over the sink. "Care to join me?" he asked, holding a bottle of whisky.

So far, everything he'd told her sounded believable, even that part about Adella being alive the last time he saw her. But she kept her eyes on him, not willing to let her guard down yet.

"No, water for me," she replied.

When he returned to the table, he placed a glass of water in front of her and then cradled a large glass of whisky as he regarded her from his position across the table.

"I'm not supposed to be drinking," he said, raising his glass with a grim smile. "Bad for my heart. That's funny when you think about it because so many people say I don't have one."

When Veronika didn't respond, he shrugged and took a drink.

"It lasted for about a month. I'd meet her on the beach at night. A few times she took me to her house when her husband was out." He took a sip of whisky, then another. "Being in her house, the place where she lived with her husband, it ate away at me. She kept talking about getting away. Erratic stuff about someone following her and how she'd die if she stayed in Seabreak."

"She told you someone was following her," Veronika said. "Did she say who?"

"No. But it was too much. I'd had enough. Yes, I was selfish. But I started to believe the things people said about her being crazy."

Veronika wrote down the word crazy. Bob Culla and Dave from the mini-mart both said Adella had lots of male friends. Adella's own sister admitted that she was depressed and a heavy drinker, but no one said anything about crazy.

"That last night," he said, looking off towards the kitchen, avoiding Veronika's eyes, "we had sex in the dunes. And then I told her it was over. It was a shitty thing to do, and it's no excuse, but I was a kid."

It *was* a shitty thing to do to a woman he believed to be in a fragile mental state. But it seemed *some* of the men in Seabreak preyed on Adella's fragility while others turned a blind eye to what was happening. People who probably knew the woman before she suffered a life-changing brain injury. The idea sickened Veronika, but she forced her expression to remain impassive.

"Anyway," he continued, "she exploded, hitting me and screaming, hurling abuse. She scratched me across the neck. Christ, I just wanted to get away. I pushed her, and she fell back onto the sand. She called me a coward. She was right, I was a coward. I am a coward. I turned and ran. That was the last time I saw her, she was angry, but she was very much alive."

Veronika wasn't sure if she believed him. But he could have kept it all to himself and refused to speak to her, yet he'd admitted to being the last person to see Adella before she vanished. Either he was playing games with her or Richard Wilson was telling the truth. There was no denying he was a selfish asshole, but was he a truthful one?

"You think that's what Jane heard?" she asked. "You and Adella arguing?"

He shrugged. "But Jane saw someone choking Adella. That wasn't me. I don't know who it was."

Veronika thought for a moment. Jane, Adella and Richard; a circle with a missing piece. Something didn't make sense.

"There's something else," he said. "Jane thought Adella called out a word when she was being attacked. *Bitch.* I think Jane got that part wrong. I've had years to think about this, and I believe Adella was calling for help. You see, Adella always called me Rich." He took another drink. A deep swallow. "She was calling out Rich."

"You say you left her alive. Yet when you found out she was missing, you didn't come forward," Veronika pointed out.

"I know," he snapped. "Don't you think I know? But I didn't know she'd been murdered, not then. I thought she'd killed herself. What good would it have done if I got involved? If I'd said anything, I'd have been dragging my father and brother into the whole mess. You don't know what small towns are like, Inspector. I was leaving Seabreak in a few weeks, going back to uni. What good would it have done if I admitted to having an affair with a married woman?"

"And when your wife told you she'd seen Adella being murdered?" Veronika asked.

He took another drink and grimaced. "I didn't believe the two events were related. Adella's murder and Jane's disappearance. How could they be?" Richard's eyes were bleary and starting to lose focus. "And then there was Bob Culla. That prick all but called me a murderer. He had his mind made up from the moment he saw me. He never liked my father, always had it in for him."

He was halfway to being drunk. His mind was jumping from one thing to the next. If he kept going, she'd lose him and this could be her only chance to get to the truth. Tomorrow, he might wake up with a clear head and rethink his story. Or, the rapid drinking was a smart move. He could tell his story and still have deniability if things went the wrong way.

"You said Culla," Veronika pointed out. "Don't you mean Bender?"

"Bender," he scoffed. "He went on whatever Culla fed him. And they had me in their sights. I wasn't about to tell them Jane was the second woman I'd been with just before she disappeared. They would have crucified me." He pointed an unsteady finger in Veronika's direction. "They tried to crucify me." He laughed. "I don't know why I'm telling you, you're one of them."

So Culla started the witch hunt. She wasn't surprised he'd distanced himself from the case once things went sideways for Bender. A smart move, but also one that spoke to the man's character.

"Listen," Veronika said. "I'm trying to get to the truth. I couldn't give a toss what Culla and Bender thought. Just slow down on the whisky."

He paused with the glass halfway to his mouth. Behind his spectacles, his eyelids were drooping.

"Did anyone know about you and Adella?" she asked.

"My old man suspected something. He saw the scratch on me the next morning, but Edward covered for me. He said we got into a fight. We were always fighting and making up," he said, words slurring. "We always covered for each other. He's a good brother, you know." As he spoke, a tear rolled down his cheek. "I should treat him better.

"When news broke about Adella going missing," he continued, "my father looked at me like I was a monster. But Ed kept backing me up. Things were never the same after that. Not between me and Dad. Not with me and Ed."

A minute later, he was running for the bathroom. He must have cut it close to the bone because he didn't stop to close the door and the sound of him retching his guts up echoed through the apartment.

"Great," Veronika said to herself and closed her notebook.

When she left, Richard was on the couch snoring.

Chapter Thirty-one

Once she was in the car, Veronika checked her phone. A missed call and a text from Jim. Maybe she wasn't the only one who had new information. When she returned the call, a woman answered.

"DI Pope? This is Sergeant Margaret Nuse."

Veronika's stomach dropped. There was no *good* reason why someone else would answer Jim's phone. "What's happened?" Veronika asked, her heart pounding.

They spoke for a few minutes before Veronika hung up, called Stacey, and then drove out of the parking lot.

* * *

She'd been to Jim's house countless times, but when she pulled up, her gut was in knots.

Julie answered the door with a toddler on her hip. When she saw Veronika, she smiled and then realisation clicked, and her expression changed to fear.

"Oh God, no," Julie said and started backing up, looking for a way of escaping.

"It's not that," Veronika hurriedly said. "He's hurt, but okay."

"Tell me?" Julie demanded, still blocking the door while Amelie sucked her index finger and looked from her mother to Veronika.

Perhaps hearing panic in her owner's voice, Hope – Jim and Julie's golden retriever – barked and appeared at the door.

"Can I come in first?" Veronika asked, more concerned for Julie, who looked wobbly. "You look like you need to sit. I know I do."

Julie seemed about to argue, but turned and led Veronika into the sitting room. She set Amelie down on the floor, but remained standing.

"Where is he, Veronika?"

"He's still in Seabreak, in the infirmary," she replied, seating herself on the sofa. "He's going to be fine. Now please sit for a second." She patted the seat next to her.

Julie wavered but acquiesced and flopped onto the sofa. "Christ, Veronika, I've dreaded this day. I try to put on a brave face, but I'm always waiting for that knock on the door."

"He was hit with a bottle and lost consciousness. It happened this morning when he was questioning a witness. He's in the local hospital." Julie started to stand, but Veronika took hold of her hand. "Just listen. He's had a scan and everything is fine. They're keeping him in overnight for observation. I spoke to the sergeant in charge up there and she said Jim is going to call you as soon as he's back in his room."

"I should call my mum, ask her to look after Amelie," Julie said. "It will be easier if I go alone–"

"I'm headed that way this afternoon to check on a few witnesses," Veronika interrupted. It was a half-truth. In fact, she'd only decided to return to Seabreak after she spoke to Sergeant Nuse. "I can take Jim a change of clothes and bring him home in the morning."

Before Julie could respond, her phone rang, and she jumped up and rushed into the kitchen to answer it. Left alone with the baby, Veronika let out a long breath and tipped her head back until she could see the ceiling. Jim would be fine, at least that's what Margaret Nuse had said, but she was no doctor. A head injury, it made her think of Adella Reece's sister's words. *When she came out of that coma, something dark had attached itself to her.* It was an overreaction; Jim wasn't in a coma. His injuries were nowhere near as traumatic as Adella's. Veronika didn't know why she was making comparisons.

"Da?" Amelie said, smiling up at Veronika as she struggled to stand on her chubby legs.

"He'll be home tomorrow," Veronika replied, going over to the baby and sitting on the floor in front of her.

Veronika smiled and offered the toddler her hands. Amelie happily took hold and used them for support as she clamoured to her feet.

"That was Jim," Julie said, returning from the kitchen. She sniffed and ran her hands through her blonde hair. "He sounds okay. He wants me to stay here, so I will. But I don't like it. If I wasn't so relieved, I'd drive to Seabreak just to tell him off for scaring me."

"Happy to do that for you?" Veronika offered and then chuckled when Amelie grasped her nose in her chubby little fist.

"I'll have him back to you and this precious little one tomorrow morning," Veronika said, manoeuvring her nose out of Amelie's grasp.

"Will it ever stop?" Julie asked. "The worry, the dread?"

Veronika felt for her. How could she not? Her own family had asked the same questions. And Jim, when he got home, might have bigger issues than a sore head to reconcile.

"We work cold cases," Veronika said, getting up from the floor. "Less risk – usually. And, the higher Jim rises, the less chance of something like this happening. Less time alone and out of the office. I spend most of my time talking to witnesses. On the phone, following leads."

As she dropped her pearls of wisdom, she thought of Richard Wilson and the moment it seemed like he was about to confess to murder. Cold case, high rank, none of it mattered in that moment when she thought she might have to fight for her life. In truth, there was no telling when anyone working a case would find themselves in the midst of a shitstorm.

"Thanks," Julie said, and squeezed Veronika's arm. "I'll go pack Jim a change of clothes."

* * *

She stopped at home long enough to grab a change of clothes and a few essentials and book herself a room at the Seabreak pub.

"It's moving day tomorrow," her mother said, following her to the car. "Tony and Verity are having lunch here before taking the last of his stuff."

"Damn," Veronika said, dumping her bag in the boot.

How had it slipped her mind? A few days ago, she could think of nothing else *but* Tony moving out.

"I'll be back by lunchtime," she said. "I'll pick up some steaks on my way home. We can crank up the barbie."

Mary-Lynn looked doubtful. "You need to be here," she said, following her daughter to the driver's door.

"I will," Veronika said, climbing behind the wheel. "I'll grab dessert too."

The drive was tedious and, less than an hour out of the city, the radio station sputtered into static and dropped out completely. But she was grateful for the time to think. Richard, if he was telling the truth, had filled in some of the gaps, but she was still no closer to finding out who killed Adella – and Jane.

Jason Reece's alibi was solid, but she suspected he knew something that ultimately cost him his life. Whoever silenced him knew reopening the Jane Wilson case might lead to Adella.

Richard said his brother knew about his affair with Adella and covered for him. Maybe when Richard told his brother about the renewed investigation, Edward decided he needed to keep covering for him. Could it be that Edward went as far as killing Jason to keep him from talking to the police?

When Stacey interviewed Veeta Seckov, she described her attacker as an older Australian. Someone strong. The scant description definitely fit Edward Wilson – and half the men in Western Australia. Or maybe Veronika was way off.

When she reached the sign for Seabreak, she pulled over and called Brian.

"Fill me in on the psych?" she asked.

"Still playing innocent," Brian replied. "Doesn't know anything, didn't do anything."

"Not surprising," she said. "Physically, how would you describe him?"

"On the small side," Brian said. "Think weasel."

Before she hung up, he asked, "How's Jim?"

She recounted what she'd told Jim's wife, adding, "He took a nasty blow to the head and then hit the other side on a table on the way down. I'm on my way to check on him." She looked at her watch. "I'll be there by late afternoon."

"Anything I can do?" he asked.

"See what you can find on Bob Culla, but be discrete."

"You think he's involved?"

She couldn't blame Brian for sounding surprised. "Probably not," she replied. "But take a look, anyway."

She drove straight to the hospital, if you could call it that. The Seabreak Infirmary, a 1960s red-brick building next to a weatherboard chapel, reminded her of an old-fashioned orphanage. When she pulled over near the entrance, she half-expected to see nuns wandering the grounds.

Once inside the main door, she was relieved to find the walls were painted in a calming shade of periwinkle blue and the reception desk manned, not by an ageing nun, but a business-like woman with her hair in a shiny ponytail.

Of the ten double rooms allocated to inpatients, Veronika was directed to the one at the far end of the corridor. Before entering, it occurred to her that she should have brought something more than Jim's overnight bag. Grapes, perhaps, or was that too much of a cliché? Why was it that hospital stays and fruit were so tightly aligned?

Seeing Jim propped up on the pillows with his face swollen, bruised and partially covered with dressings, all thoughts of grapes faded.

"Hi," she said in an overly cheerful voice, and winced internally. "How's your head?" she asked, switching gears and trying to lighten the mood.

"No complaints so far," he replied, and grimaced. "I'm fine. Banged up, but I'll live."

"Julie packed a bag," she said, looking for a place to set the carryall down. "When they release you in the morning, I'll drive you home."

"How is she?" he asked.

Veronika sat. "Worried. Angry. Scared. All of the above. She has a right to be. She just wants you back and in one piece. All this scared the hell out of her."

"I don't know how I let it happen," he said, touching a finger to the dressing over his eye. "I could see the bloke was drunk and looking for someone to blame. I should have waited for him to sober up, or at least kept my guard up. Kept my distance."

"We've all been there," she said. "In the moment. Too focused on one thing and not enough on the other. Trust me, it happens to the best of us."

She didn't have to spell it out. They both knew a poor decision in their job could cost you everything.

He leaned back into the pillows. She could see he was struggling with a myriad of emotions. A violent attack will do that, knock the wind out and leave you as raw as your wounds.

"It might be our unidentified subject," Jim said, changing the subject after a few minutes of silence. "Ashley Simcock, I think it might be him."

Veronika wanted to tell him to rest, think about anything but the case, but if he was correct, she couldn't allow him that luxury.

"There were signs of a struggle," he continued. "If he did murder Jason Reece, that means he was in the area *and* still capable of killing. He could be back to his old modus operandi."

She thought the same thing. And, as heinous as it was, if the man was still active, it would be easier to catch him.

Veronika filled him in on her meeting with Richard Wilson. "He confirmed what we suspected about Jane witnessing Adella's murder."

Before she could say more, her phone rang. It was Stacey.

"Stacey hasn't heard from the local police on Mrs Campion's noise complaint," Veronika said to Jim after ending the call. "We have Richard's word on when Jane was in Seabreak as a kid. I'd like definitive confirmation."

"You think he's lying?" Jim asked.

Veronika took a moment before answering. She could usually get a beat on a person within minutes, but Richard was hard to read.

"I'm not sure," she replied. "He goes from robotic to emotional in a heartbeat. He seemed to be deliberately getting drunk while speaking to me. I'm still on the fence when it comes to Richard *and* the brother."

"See Madge Nuse," Jim offered. "If it's on file, she'll find it."

"Madge?" Veronika said, suppressing a smile.

Jim laughed, then winced. "I know, but she's okay."

Before she left, Veronika pulled out her phone and brought up the photo of Adella and Jason in happier times.

"See this fence in the background?" She showed him the phone. "Did you see anything like this around town?"

"No, but you could–"

"I know," she replied. "Ask Madge. I will. Get some rest. I'll be back bright and early."

On her way to the police station, Veronika passed the mini-mart. On impulse, she slowed, pulled a U-turn and then parked in front of the shop.

Dave looked up from his newspaper. "Inspector Pope, I thought you'd be back in the big smoke by now."

"I was," she replied. "But I had a few things to attend to, and I thought of you."

"Now, Inspector," he said, holding his hands up, "I'm a married man."

She couldn't help smiling. "You're breaking my heart, Dave." She pulled out her phone. "Do you recognise this fence?" she asked, showing him the photo of Adella and Jason.

"Can you make it bigger?" he asked.

Veronika zoomed in on the area over Adella's shoulder and handed the phone to him. Dave took it and squinted at the screen.

"I can't be sure," he said, handing it back, "but it looks like the fence out the front of Lester's place."

"Lester West?"

"You know him?" Dave asked, surprised.

"What can you tell me about him?" she asked, ignoring his question.

He looked doubtful, as though he was about to say something, but then changed his mind. "He owns the petrol station. Lived in Seabreak all his life. That there" – he pointed to the phone – "was Lester's father's house.

The business too. He's a bit, um, crusty, if you know what I mean."

Crusty. It was a nice way of saying Lester was an ill-tempered dickhead. At least, that was Veronika's experience with the man.

"The house is on Bushnell Road," Dave added. "Don't know what number."

Veronika tucked her phone away and thanked him. As she was about to leave, he stopped her.

"Is it anything to do with this?" Dave asked, holding up the newspaper so she could see the front page.

The one-word headline read: *Missing*. Below it was a half-page image of a young woman with long red hair. Veronika took the paper and scanned the article detailing Ashley Simcock's disappearance.

Was it linked to her case, she wondered. The more they dug into Adella and Jane, the greater the chances were that they were dealing with a serial offender. "No, just a few loose ends on another case," she said.

"This girl, she's around the same age as my granddaughter. What I don't understand is why." He looked at the newspaper and Ashley Simcock's happy, youthful face. "Why would someone take a girl and hurt her? Steal her away from her family? Cause so much misery."

Veronika didn't have an answer, not a good one. Even if she caught whoever was responsible, there would never be a definitive answer. People would speculate, but that's all it would be, speculation. She'd seen enough to know that some individuals' minds were unfathomable. There were voids where kindness and conscience didn't exist. A person's inner nature, that essence that made them who they are, was a secret inscape. The man they were looking for, his inscape was a dark and twisted wasteland.

"I wish I knew, Dave," she said, heading for the door.

Chapter Thirty-two

Sometimes it was hard to control his breathing. It came too fast, his chest bouncing with the force of keeping up with his lungs. Other times, the air slithered out of him like a night crawler caught in the sun. With the wind pestering the old gutters and whispering around the eaves, he felt himself falling back in time. Back to a time when his brother would sleep deeply on the other side of the room.

His brother was always a good sleeper. The voices, the scrape of furniture being shoved, the screams, were lost on him. Not so for *him*. When his parents started up with the arguing, he'd wake with a gasp and listen to the vicious words, the loud struggles and the begging and crying.

With sweat clinging to his face and neck, he'd leave his bed and creep downstairs so he could sit on the floor, watching his parents' shadows through the crack of the door.

He was doing things that summer. Bad things. Crawling on his belly like a snake through the dunes so he could watch people. So he could see the stuff they did when they thought no one was watching. He'd dream about the things he saw. It was always his mother's face on the women's necks.

In the daylight, they all went about the house in silence, mostly. In the day, the place smelled like cigarettes and stale sweat. But, at night, they lived out their secret horror show. If he watched, stayed awake and listened, he could will the night to end and the daytime silence to return. Silence was safer. Even the lingering stench of the night's horror was bearable.

That night, so many years ago, still lived within the walls of the family house. He remembered they were upstairs. He slid down the wall and pulled the door ajar so he could see them on the landing. She spat hateful words. His mother had a talent for hate. His father, so strong and silent, would sob like a baby – and beg.

He detested his mother with all the force of his love. Her poison was infecting him. He could feel it pumping through him like oily venom. He both pitied and loathed his father for his weakness. For letting her bring him so low. A monster walked the house at night, but until *that* night, he'd never seen its face.

"Who is he?" his father begged. "Is it worth it? What you're doing to me, to the boys?"

"Is it worth it?" she mimicked. "Yes, it's worth it. I'd let a dog lick me before I'd let you touch me. And I *need* touching." She laughed, pleased with the cruelty of her words. "The boys, the boys. You don't care about me, just your precious boys. I'll take him and go. How would you like that?"

"You're not taking him." His father sounded stronger, angry. "He needs help and he won't get it from you."

He was fourteen, just a kid sitting in the door's crack with his knees pressed against his chest, but he knew she meant it. The thought of leaving his father and brother made his heart pound. He clenched his fists and shoved one into his mouth. She'd never talked about taking him before. But she could, he realised. And what of his father's words? *He needs help.*

"He's mine," she shrieked. "You can't stop me."

He glanced back at the bed where his brother was still breathing softly in his sleep. How was it possible that he could sleep on when their world was being torn to shreds?

"You're drunk. I'm going to bed," his father said. There was no strength in his voice, no hope.

"Fuck you," she spat. "Maybe we'll be gone when you wake up."

He heard his father close the bedroom door. He must have locked it, shutting her out. She thumped on the wood with her fist. "I'll take him and you'll never see us again."

He could see her clearly now, her naked body visible under the filmy nightie. Her form, so clearly female, sickened him. He didn't know he was going to move until he was on the landing and his hands were around her throat.

She smelt like booze and cigarettes and her skin felt frail under his fingers.

"You slut." He heard the words coming out of his mouth and liked them. They had been stuck in his throat for so long, setting them free made him shudder with pleasure.

Her eyes bulged with fear, reminding him of a beached blowfish as she batted at him with clawed hands. She wasn't scoffing now. Nor was she talking about taking him or hurling vile words. She looked terrified, and the sight of her fear made him insane with joy.

"Stop, stop. Let her go." His father was behind him, pulling him off her. "Don't, son. Don't do it. You're not thinking straight."

When his father finally got him off her, she coughed and gagged. Still at the top of the stairs, one hand to her neck, she pointed at him as though he were a freak. A horrifying apparition that only she could see.

The heat of her skin was still on his palms, burning into him. And she kept pointing and gagging. His father released his grip so he could go to her, but *he* was faster.

All it took was a push. A jab to the chest and she was gone.

Her body hit the stairs and folded on itself, going over like a bony slinky, cracking and crumpling. That fall went on and on as if the stairs had become a deep cavern and his mother a hiker plummeting into its depths.

Behind him, his father called her name and rushed for the stairs. Somehow, amidst the chaos, his brother finally awoke and stood at his shoulder.

"She fell," his father said at the bottom of the stairs, cradling her head. "She fell. It was an accident."

He looked away from his parents and caught sight of the mirror on the landing. The one framed with little metal swirls in the shape of hearts. That was the first time he caught sight of the monster. He liked it.

Chapter Thirty-three

"How is he?" Nuse asked, leading Veronika into her office, where she took a seat behind the desk and swivelled a worn leather chair in Veronika's direction.

Sergeant Nuse was a solid-looking woman with broad hands and laugh lines at the corner of her eyes. With her impeccably pressed uniform and tight bun, she gave the impression of efficiency and authority. But Veronika suspected there was a sense of humour under all that starch.

"Banged up. He'll heal, but it will leave a nasty scar," Veronika replied, taking a seat. "He'll be better when I get him home."

"Jim's a good bloke, a smart detective. He'd do well in country policing, if what happened in Ledge Point doesn't put him off."

Veronika couldn't imagine Jim as a small-town cop, but maybe Nuse saw something in him she didn't.

"We've charged Evan Malacci with aggravated assault on a public officer," Nuse continued. "He's the worst kind of drunk; a mean one. He was half cut, but he knew what he was doing." She leaned her elbows on the desk. "I saw him lift that bottle, spotted it out of the corner of my eye.

If I'd been a second quicker, I could have stopped him. When we got Jim to the hospital, the doctor said a few centimetres to the left and he would have lost his eye."

Veronika thought of Julie's face when she answered the door and saw Veronika standing there alone. The woman had thought her husband was dead. A split second was all it took and things could have gone the other way. Jim could be dead or maimed for life.

"They're sending a couple of uniforms to transport him to the city." Nuse checked her watch. "They should be here by five o'clock. Do you want to speak to him before he goes?"

Veronika shook her head. The last thing she wanted was to see the drunken shit who bashed her partner over the head. "I need the details on a noise complaint from January or February 2000."

"Go ahead," Nuse said, grabbing a pen.

Veronika gave her the name and approximate date. "We're trying to confirm a timeline. A record of the complaint will pin down one of our victim's whereabouts."

"I'll get it to you before I leave for the day. Anything else?" she asked.

"Seabreak still attracts the windsurfing crowd, right?" Veronika said.

Nuse gave a slow nod. "We still get a solid stream of them. Never understood the attraction. I saw *Jaws* when I was fourteen and it was enough to keep me on dry land for life."

"Any regulars?" Veronika asked.

"Plenty, but I couldn't name one," Nuse replied. "It's not like they check in with us. The summer crowd comes and goes."

"Any of the regulars ever cause a problem?" Veronika pushed.

She could see the other woman thinking, picking up on Veronika's line of thought. "Nothing comes to mind, but I'll check the records."

Veronika was about to stand when Nuse dropped her pen. "It's been a bastard of a day. I need a drink and you look like you could use one too. You're staying at the pub, right? The bar downstairs isn't much, but they do a mean parmy."

Veronika was exhausted, but the idea of going up to her single room over the pub with its bare light bulb and dripping tap was less than appealing. "I've got something I need to chase up first, but yes, I could use something stronger than tea. And it's been a while since I've had a decent pub meal. Thanks for the offer, Margaret."

"Call me Madge," she replied. "Care to share what you're chasing?"

"Lester West? Do you know him?"

"Nasty old bugger from the petrol station," Madge replied. "I haven't dealt with him professionally, but I've bought petrol at his place. The man has a face like a well-smacked bum."

It was a fair assessment of the man's countenance, one that made Veronika chuckle.

"He's not exactly a ray of sunshine, but I think he might have known one of the missing women we're investigating. I doubt he can add anything, but it's worth a try." Veronika paused, wondering how much she should reveal. "I'm also thinking of dropping in on Edward Wilson, just to clear a few things up."

"I thought inspectors usually have someone chauffeuring them around," Madge said.

"So, they tell me," Veronika replied wryly.

"Tell you what," Madge said. "I'll grab a booth at the pub and save you a seat. It's 4:00 p.m. now. If you're not there by 5:30 p.m., I'll send out a search party."

Madge cracked a smile that didn't quite reach her eyes. Veronika thought the woman was only half joking about the search party.

* * *

Judging by the look of resignation on Edward's face, he wasn't surprised to see her. The look told her he'd spoken to his brother. She could only imagine how *that* conversation went; Richard waking up late afternoon, hung-over and possibly vague on what exactly he'd told her. Ringing his twin in a panic.

"Come in," Edward said, holding the door open for her. Not exactly a welcome wagon, but a big turnaround from the last time she'd showed up on his doorstep.

After her chat with his brother, she had her doubts about Edward and intended to tread carefully. "Out here will do," Veronika replied, indicating to the small porch area.

The late afternoon sun was on the downward, leaving the front of the house in shadows. Not the most inviting place for a chat about murder, but it was more appealing than stepping into the man's house.

A look crossed his face; disappointment? Confusion? She wasn't sure, but the doubt confirmed her instinct to talk outside.

"Suit yourself," he muttered, stepping over the threshold. "But make it quick–"

"Yes," she cut him off. "I know, you're very busy. But what I have to say is important, so *make* time."

His chin tightened, and it looked like he wanted to argue, but thought better of it.

"Your brother," she began. "He has added some new information to his account of the night his wife went missing. So now it's your turn to give me your version of events."

It was a vague request, almost an accusation. What she was doing was risky, but she wanted Edward to be unsure about how much she knew. She wanted him to question his hungover brother's memory of the things he'd revealed.

"My version?" he repeated with what sounded like indignation.

"Richard said, on the night his wife went missing, she confided in him about something that happened in Seabreak in 2000. A woman who both you and your brother knew went missing," Veronika continued. "You were the only other person in the house the night Jane told Richard about the things she'd witnessed. Did you hear any of that conversation?"

"I was asleep," he snapped. "I told Culla all this, and now I'm telling you."

"But you know what they talked about." It was a statement, not a question.

"It doesn't matter what they talked about," he said, planting his hands on his hips. "My brother did nothing wrong."

"Which time are you talking about?" Edward was tall, over six feet, but she held her ground *and* his gaze. "The night Adella or Jane went missing?"

He came towards her and she braced herself, ready to kick his right leg out from under him. Instead of grabbing her, he brushed past and leaned on the weathered porch post. With his back to her, he faced the road.

"This thing never ends," he said. "It just follows us like a plague."

"It can end with the truth," she said. "Your brother said you covered for him. Did you kill Adella Reece?"

He spun around. "Is that what you think happened? You think I covered for my brother by killing Adella and then his wife? You think I'm some maniac creeping around killing people? For Christ's sake." The last words came out with an exaggerated scoffing laugh.

"Richard said you covered for each other," she persisted. "If you want this to end, tell me who's covering for who?"

He nodded, more to himself than to her. "When Richard came in that night, he was all scratched up. He told me he'd finished with Adella and she lost it and started hitting him. I told our old man that we got in a fight. We always got into it, fighting over nothing and then, as quick as it started, it was forgotten and everything was good again. I didn't want my father to know Richard had been seeing a married woman, so I lied for him. That's it."

She waited, sensing there was more.

"Richie covered for me because" – he looked away – "our father didn't know I was gay. I think he guessed – later, but not then. Then, I was living a lie.

"Fucking Culla caught me one night, not long after Adella went missing," he continued. "I was in the back seat of a car with someone, a man. I'd never been so humiliated. He made me kneel on the ground with my hands behind my head like I was a criminal. Like being gay was a crime." He stopped and seemed lost in the memory.

"And Richard," she prompted.

"Culla called the house." Edward laughed. "I was a grown man, and he tried to call my father to come and get me. He wanted to shame me and hurt my old man."

Veronika didn't know if she believed everything he was saying, but she didn't doubt the part about Culla. In her mind's eyes, she could see him behind his desk, the look of self-satisfaction on his face when he talked about Adella knowing lots of men. The way his expression changed when Veronika pushed him to answer her questions. From what Edward described, Culla was not only judgemental and egotistical but also cruel.

"He treated me like some sort of degenerate who needed someone normal to escort them home," he continued. "But Richie answered the phone. I don't know what he said to Culla, but he let me go. If Culla ever said anything to my father later, Dad never showed it."

"Did your brother tell you what he said to Culla?" she asked, genuinely curious about what Richard could have said to a man like Culla to make him change his mind.

"Just that he'd smoothed things over," Edward replied. "We didn't talk about it again. It was awkward. But, up to the day my father died, I lived in fear that Culla would get it into his head to tell him. Now, I don't give a damn who knows or what they think, including you," he said, looking down at her. "So now you know, Inspector. Is that enough for you?"

"Yes, for now," she said. Before stepping off the porch, she stopped. "I'm sorry you had to go through that, Edward. I'm grateful for your honesty."

Chapter Thirty-four

It was almost half past four when Veronika climbed behind the wheel. The sun was waning and the golden hour had begun. This was her favourite time of the day. A time when the sun is close to the horizon and its light is softer. The magical hour loved by photographers and filmmakers, also a time when all things seem possible. Golden hour was early, especially for summer, but the heat had turned from dry to humid and clouds were gathering offshore.

She peeled off her jacket and tossed it on the passenger seat, started the engine and turned up the air con. With the window half down and her blouse sticking to her skin, she waited for the cool air to drive the heat out of the cab.

Before speaking to Edward, she had a theory – one that made sense, sort of. Richard Wilson tried to end his affair with Adella. Things got physical and Richard killed Adella either accidentally or on purpose. His twin helped him get rid of the body. Maybe they took their father's boat out and dumped her a few kilometres offshore. The tide was strong and there were plenty of sharks in the water.

Then, years later, Richard marries Jane and brings her home to Seabreak. He marries the very woman who saw the murder. A coincidence or just one of those weird happenstances that occurs in an isolated place like Perth? A place where there are only three degrees of separation between complete strangers, friends of friends, and close family. In golden hour, Veronika was leaning towards the latter.

Jane tells Richard what she saw all those years before. Perhaps something sparked Jane's memory, and she recognised Richard as the man on the beach. Or Richard said something that tipped Jane off. Jane threatened to go to the police. Knowing they'd both go to prison, the brothers decided to silence her for good. Not a bad theory, but not enough flesh on its bones. Too many holes. Like how Jason Reece's apparent suicide fitted with her theory. And it wasn't just the missing pieces, Edward came across as truthful. Angry and distrusting of police, but honest.

She was still pondering Richard's account of his last night with Adella when her phone rang.

"I have the details on the noise complaint," Madge said. "The seventeenth of January 2000."

"Great," Veronika replied. "That matches up with our timeline."

"The complaint was called in by Marian Campion," she continued, "and attended by Constable Robert Culla."

Veronika thought she'd misheard the last part. "Did you say Robert Culla attended?"

"That's right," Madge said. "He was stationed here before my time."

Veronika thanked her and hung up. So Culla had met the Campions, perhaps even talked to Jane. Not that he would have put the two things together when Edward Wilson reported Jane missing. Her surname was different. Culla would have had no way of knowing it was the same person whom he might have met fifteen years earlier. But, when things got complicated and Jane's parents got involved, he would have known then.

It could have slipped his mind. So many call-outs over the years, it would be easy to forget one noise complaint. Still, it was strange. A cop with Culla's years of experience should be adept at making connections, remembering faces and names. Veronika remembered the face of every person she'd arrested and every witness she'd questioned. She couldn't call all their names to mind, but if she saw them again, it would trigger a memory. Or another possibility was that Culla remembered meeting Jane's parents and, for some reason, chose not to mention it.

The light was dying, so she set her thoughts on Culla aside, pulled up the map on her phone, and drove to Bushnell Road.

It was a quiet street, similar to the one Jason Reece lived on, only closer to the ocean. The fence wasn't hard to spot. With its curved iron railings, it stuck out amongst the beachy looking homes and reminded her of something out of Victorian London. She parked across the road, three houses back, and stared at the structure.

A large house, two storeys with a double garage attached. With the garage door down, there was no way of knowing if Lester was home, so she waited. From her position, she could see the front yard. The grass was overgrown, not the manicured lawn that Jason and Adella had once posed on. Deciding she'd waited long enough, Veronika grabbed her jacket, left the car, and approached the house.

In the dying light, there was something unsettling about the structure, with its sharp railings and unlit windows. Or perhaps the place offended her because she found its owner unpleasant. Part of her wanted to call it a day and head for the pub. If Lester did know anything, it was unlikely he'd share it with her. The brief encounter at the petrol station proved he didn't like cops.

She could always come back early in the morning before picking Jim up from the hospital. She checked her watch; ten minutes to five, plenty of time to ask Lester a few questions and still be on time for her dinner with Madge.

"Get the damn thing over with," she muttered to herself. Why not? She didn't intend to enter the building, just another chat on the porch.

Veronika paused at the front gate. The latch was rusty and looked like it hadn't been used since Adella and Jason sat for that long ago photo. Best guess was that Lester probably entered through the garage. She reached over, gave the latch a couple of twists and it grudgingly pulled back. The old ache in her shoulder pulsed, and a spike of pain radiated down her arm. It took a couple of slow shoulder rolls before the pulse eased. It was her own fault. Skipping exercise was the fastest way to a frozen shoulder.

When she pushed, the gate moved about half a metre, ploughing up sand and weeds, then stopped. Veronika gave it a shove, but all that did was drive the bottom of the thing deeper into the ground cover. Deciding the old gate wasn't going anywhere, she turned and pushed through the gap side-on, whacking her elbow on the rusty latch in the process.

By the time she stepped onto the porch and the timbers, dry as dead wood, groaned beneath her shoes, Veronika's elbow was stinging like a nest of jellyfish. There was no bell or knocker so she used her fist and rapped twice, sharp thudding raps which she hoped would echo through the house.

Silence. One more knock and she'd call it quits and go back to her room over the bar and ice her arm. To her surprise, a light appeared in the ground-floor window to her right. A moment later, the door opened.

The man in the doorway looked startled, as if she was the last person he expected to see.

Veronika couldn't keep the surprise out of her voice. "Culla?"

"Inspector, this is a surprise." The startled look vanished, and he appeared genuinely pleased to see her. "Come in."

Surprised or not, Bob Culla was a cop. A sergeant. Her asking him to step outside would seem highly unusual. And, worse, he'd see it as a sign of weakness if she hesitated. There were bigger things in life to worry about than Bob Culla's view of her, but she'd be damned if she'd let him think she was afraid of him.

"What are you doing here?" she asked, prolonging the moment, trying to find a way to extract herself from the situation.

"Just visiting my old stomping ground. In fact," he added, "I'm glad you're here." He held the door open.

"I was hoping to speak to Lester," she said, still unsure how Culla fitted in with the man from the petrol station. "Is he here?"

"No, he'll be back soon. But I think I found something that might be useful to you."

Veronika made a show of checking her watch, not really registering the time. "I have a meeting with Sergeant Nuse. I'll leave my card. Let me know when Lester turns up."

She was reaching into her back pocket when Culla shook his head. "I think you should see this for yourself." He stepped aside. She could see the sitting room behind him and noted a standing lamp next to an open carton of papers.

"After you visited me in Mandurah, I got to thinking about the case and I remembered something."

He stopped talking and waited, making it clear that if she wanted to know more, she'd have to indulge him. Was he talking about the noise complaint? She wondered if he'd checked his notes and found something. Still, he hadn't explained what he was doing in Lester's house. The situation was odd, and she didn't trust Culla, but doubted he would be a threat.

"Okay," Veronika said. "But make it quick. Nuse is expecting me."

She followed him along the hall, leaving the front door open behind her. As they passed, Veronika glanced up the staircase. The lack of light on the second storey gave the illusion of stairs leading to nowhere.

"Damn that wind," Culla said, moving past her and back to the front door. "There's a storm coming. If I leave it open, the gusts will take it off the hinges."

When he returned, he motioned for her to sit. She did, but stayed perched on the edge of the sofa. The situation felt ten kinds of strange as did seeing Culla, out of uniform, dressed in khaki pants and a T-shirt, appearing overly at home in Lester's house.

"So, what did you want to show me?" she asked. While the most obvious question was what the hell was he doing here, her gut told her to go easy and see where this was going.

Culla stood beside the armchair, looking down at the box of papers. Behind him, she could see what looked like a kitchen.

"Lester keeps so much stuff," he said absently. "What was it you wanted to ask him about?"

With his head down and the light behind him, an image jumped into her mind. *On the Beach*, the book Jane hid the newspaper clipping in; the cover art showed a man with thick blonde hair standing over a woman. The first time Veronika met Culla, she was struck by his impressive head of blonde hair and how he was only greying slightly at the temples.

Before she could answer, he turned and headed towards the kitchen. "Have a drink with me, Inspector?" he called over his shoulder.

Still thinking about the book cover, she stood and followed him to the kitchen. On the way, she paused and glanced down at what she thought was a box of papers. Photographs and drawings, bundles of them were shoved haphazardly into the carton. On top was a black-and-white photo of a family; a man, woman and two boys, one with thick blonde hair. In the background was the iron fence.

"I have whisky," Culla called from the kitchen. "Strong enough to make a rabbit spit in a bulldog's eye. That's what my old man used to say. I say my old man, but he was my stepfather."

She entered the kitchen in time to see him lifting two glasses of whisky.

"Not for me," she said. "I'm still on the clock."

"When did that ever stop anyone?" he replied with a conspiratorial grin. It was an unappealing expression that made her want to shudder.

"I'm on duty and driving," she said, reaching into her back pocket. "I'll leave my card. Get Lester to call me in the morning."

The grin disappeared. "You're bleeding."

For a second, she was confused by his response.

"Your arm." He gestured with the glasses still in his hands. "It's bleeding. You've hurt yourself."

Veronika touched her right elbow and felt a tear in her sleeve. When she looked, her fingers were coated with blood. She heard a drip and thought of the tap drip-dropping into the sink at the pub. When she looked down, there was blood on the cracked linoleum.

"Jesus," Culla said, and set one glass on the kitchen table. "Take your jacket off."

Stunned by the amount of blood on the floor, she pulled off her jacket and found that her arm was slick with blood. There was a gash just above her elbow, deep with the skin torn in a jagged line.

"I must have caught it on the gate," she said, still staring at the wound.

With her shoulder playing up, she'd attributed the pain to the old injury.

"Sit down," Culla said, concerned. "You can't go like that. At least let me put something on it."

He was right. There was no point in arguing. She couldn't drive off with her arm dripping like a handful of ice cream on a summer's day. For some reason, the blood was making her think of the beach.

"You're going to need stitches," he continued, peering at the wound. "At least five and probably a tetanus shot. That gate's rusty as hell. There's a first aid kit in the back room. I'll bandage you up and drive you to the hospital."

She wasn't squeamish, but the sight of the jagged wound and something white and shiny winking from beneath the exposed tissue made her head swim.

"Sit down," Culla said, putting a hand on her shoulder and forcing her onto a chair. "And drink that whisky. You look like you're in shock. It will help," he added, softening his tone.

Gingerly, she let her injured arm rest on her thigh. First Jim, now this. She wasn't superstitious, but it felt like Seabreak was a cursed town. As another wave of wooziness threatened to swamp her, she eyed the whisky. It probably wouldn't do much apart from easing the pain. Maybe that was a good thing because her elbow felt like it was on fire.

She picked up the glass and noticed her hands were shaking. Veronika swore under her breath and took a few deep swallows, then shuddered as the heat travelled down her throat.

The door to the back room was open, and she saw a wall with various tools on hooks. She could hear Culla moving around. Of all the places to be and the people to be with, she had to end up in Culla's lap when she was injured. If she didn't feel so light-headed, she'd wrap her jacket around her arm and run.

"Damn it," she muttered, finding it difficult to make her lips move.

He reappeared with a bottle of something, a bandage, and some gauze. When he pushed the door wider, she noticed something else hanging on the wall in the back room. Something important, but her thoughts were turning to mush and she couldn't find the words.

"This will sting," he said, pouring the liquid onto her wound.

She let out a hiss of agony as the liquid burned the exposed tissue. Instead of settling, the burning grew until she was biting her lip to hold back a scream.

"Got to make sure it's clean," he continued, pressing something against her arm.

She was barely aware of what he was doing to her arm because her limbs and head were growing numb. Numb was good, the burning faded. From where she had placed her jacket on the table, her phone vibrated.

"Rope," she mumbled and reached for her jacket, fumbling the phone out of the pocket.

Culla took the phone out of her hand and tossed it on the table. "You don't look so good, Inspector," he said, crouching in front of her.

His face floated in and out of her field of vision and his smiling mouth seemed to grow until it was as wide as a clown's. Before everything went dark, Veronika lifted her head and focused on the coil of orange rope hanging from a hook in the back room.

Chapter Thirty-five

Brian didn't go through the ordinary channels. What he was looking for wouldn't show up on a search engine or database. Veronika asked him to see what he could find on Sergeant Robert Culla. She also asked for discretion.

Amanda Raines, a senior constable and classmate from Brian's days in the academy, was a woman with connections. She was also one with a pretty face, a mind that worked at racehorse speed, a talent for disarming the most guarded soul and a quick temper. The quick temper was where Brian came in. Because of it, she owed him a favour.

"Robert Culla," Amanda repeated the name. "Give me a few hours and I'll get back to you."

She didn't bother asking questions. Brian would have been surprised if she had.

True to her word, she came back with a name. "Philip Olsen," she said when she rang back. "He's out, but willing to meet with you."

By out, they both understood she meant Olsen had been, but was no longer, a cop.

"He did a bit of time undercover. It messed him up, but he's okay," she continued.

Amanda gave Brian a time and place. Before hanging up, she said, "Don't be a stranger."

"Take care, Amanda," he replied.

* * *

Philip Olsen worked as a tyre fitter in Osborne Park. When Brian pulled around the back of the fitter's shop, he saw a man in his late thirties who matched the description Amanda had given, smoking a cigarette and leaning against a skip bin.

The man watched Brian step out of the car through a haze of smoke. With the sleeves of his overalls rolled up, Brian could see his arms were covered with tattoos. "You Brian?" he asked.

Brian had a sudden sense that he'd stepped out of reality and into a hard-boiled 1940s detective novel. The whole thing seemed a bit cloak and dagger, but Amanda had a way of doing things that always involved taking the crooked road.

Brian nodded. "You know Robert Culla?"

"Are you with the Rat Squad?" the man asked. "I don't care either way, just want to know who I'm dealing with."

He was referring to the Police Conduct Investigation Unit, commonly referred to within the force as the Rat Squad.

"No," Brian replied. "Special Crime Squad."

Olsen whistled. "What's Special Crime want with Culla?"

"Just checking him out for a friend," Brian answered. "Have you got anything?"

"Not directly, but I was involved with something when I was undercover." He took the cigarette out of his mouth and inspected the glowing tip. "Amanda says you're okay, so I'm going to tell you what I know. You can do what you want with it, but keep my name out."

Brian waited.

"A couple of blokes I was knocking around with in Mandurah introduced me to a girl," Olsen began. "Lacy Walmer. An okay kid, but on the slide. Always hooking up with guys who treated her like shit. One night, she calls one of the guys and we all go pick her up from a car park in Falcon. She didn't say what she was doing there and none of us asked. Sometimes it's better not to know."

He flicked the smoke to the concrete and stomped it with his boot. "She was a mess, crying and shaking. A cop, she said, had stopped her on the street. He was in uniform but not driving a squad car or wagon. He didn't give her his name. Hassled her. The usual stuff, only things got rough. Lacy said he threw her on the ground and started choking her."

"Jesus," Brian said, shocked. He had a good idea where this was going and what the implications would be.

"Yeah," Olsen said. "Another car came along and the cop hauled her to her feet and made a big show of reading her the riot act. *I'm letting you off with a warning*, that sort of thing. When we got there, she was terrified, and the cop was long gone. The guys I was with didn't give much of a shit what happened to Lacy. They hated cops, and this guy just gave them another reason."

"So how can you be sure it was Culla?" Brian asked.

Olsen pulled out his smokes and stuck another one between his lips. "Thing was, Lacy was seventeen, so I had to do something. It took a bit of convincing, but I got her to go with me to Mandurah Police Station the next night and sit in the car watching the cops going in and out. I was taking a risk, a big one. I was undercover, but she was a kid. She even had a stupid pink unicorn tattoo on her shoulder, for Christ's sake.

"We sat there for more than an hour. She was a bag of nerves. Every time a uniform went in or out, she looked like she might vomit or tear the car door open and start running. She didn't want to be there, can't blame her.

Anyway, Culla came outside, talking to a couple of guys in a patrol car. Lacy identified him."

"What did you do?" Brian asked.

"Nothing – then," he replied. "I wasn't scheduled to check in for another couple of days. When I finally told my boss about what happened to Lacy and described the officer, I got a name; Culla."

"And?" Brian pushed.

"And I was told it would be looked into, but I know a brush-off when I hear one."

"So, the girl's name was Lacy Walmer." Brian took out his notebook and made a note of the name. "How long ago?"

"Three years," Olsen said.

"Do you think she'd be willing to talk to me about what happened? Make a statement?"

"That's just it," Olsen replied. "She took off. About six weeks later, she was gone. Someone said she'd gone to Katanning. Maybe the thing with Culla scared her straight, but who knows? By then, I was sick of the job. Lacy was the beginning of the end for me." He pushed off the skip bin. "All I know is Culla is as twisted as they come and he's still wearing the uniform. Me, I'm glad to be out."

* * *

Brian put the phone down and rubbed his eyes. It was five o'clock, and Veronika wasn't answering.

"This is weird," Stacey said from her desk. "First Jim gets hurt and now the boss isn't picking up. What's going on in that town?"

"I'll try the local cop shop," Brian said. "You two may as well go home. No point in all of us hanging around."

He saw Stacey and Haru exchange a look. None of them wanted to say it, but it wasn't like Veronika to go off the radar for more than half an hour.

"I've got reports to finish," Stacey said, not even glancing at her laptop.

"I'm not finished with the list," Haru said. "A few more possible incidents in Two Rocks."

Brian picked up the phone and put in a call to Seabreak Police Station. After a brief conversation with a public servant running dispatch, he was put through to a Constable Wexler.

"There was an inspector in here earlier," the constable said. "She was talking to Sergeant Nuse, but I don't know where she is now."

"Can you ask her if she knows anything?" Brian replied.

"Who?" Wexler asked. "The inspector or the sergeant?"

Brian pinched the bridge of his nose with his thumb and forefinger and closed his eyes. "Your sergeant," Brian said slowly. "Can you ask her if she knows where DI Pope is?"

"Oh, right," the young man replied. "She's just left for the day."

"Okay," Brian responded, willing himself to stay calm. "Can you give me the sergeant's number?"

When he finally hung up, he noticed both Stacey and Haru watching him.

"I don't remember ever being that young," he mumbled and punched in Sergeant Nuse's number.

Chapter Thirty-six

Veronika shifted, and the darkness started to clear. Pain, ceaseless burning agony, jarred her out of sleep. Not sleep, too black and empty to be sleep. The weight of her limbs and the contrast between light and dark made her think of unconsciousness. A word that swam to the surface of her thoughts and then dived out of reach.

She was aware of something hard and flat under her cheek. Of her body slumped and her shoulders raised painfully above her head. She wanted to curl back into the darkness. Her eyelids opened then drifted down, but pain and noise jolted her back.

At first, Veronika thought she was in her room above the bar with the constant dripping tap, but this was different. The drip had multiplied and hardened. Rain. There was something else. Murmuring. She forced her lids to open and realised that the world was askew and the murmuring was voices. One voice she recognised: Culla.

The name galvanised her, and she lifted her head. The world wasn't slanted; she was slumped across a table, arms above her head. With her head raised slightly, the kitchen came into focus and with it, memories barrelled towards her like a picture show in reverse.

Lester West's house, Bob Culla, her arm and the drink – the orange rope. Culla had put something in her drink. She remembered the wound on her elbow and the blood dripping down her arm, not enough blood to drag her into unconsciousness. He'd drugged her.

Determined to move, she raised her head and saw a bottle on the table. A plastic one litre bottle. Her eyes were bleary, but by squinting she could read the label: bleach. Culla had poured something on her wound. Something that burned not like antiseptic, but with a fire that kept boring into her flesh. Bleach, she could smell it on her skin and in the air.

The voices were louder. Two men. Drawing back, she tried to pull herself up, but her left shoulder was locked. She had no option but to push up on her right. When she moved, her hand slipped, but she gripped the edge of the table and found purchase.

"No, you're out of your mind."

She stopped and listened. It wasn't Culla's voice. It had to be Lester West.

"It won't work, not with a cop. They'll have half the state out looking for her."

"Including me," Culla came back. "I know what I'm doing. It'll work."

"No." West's voice was an angry rumble. "No more, Bob. Not right after the last one."

She heard heavy footfalls, and the knob rattled behind her. Veronika flung herself back onto the table just as the door opened.

They were in the room with her, less than a metre away.

"We're in this together," Culla snapped. "Do you want to go to prison? For her? I've seen those places and, Les, you won't survive a month."

"We're not together," West barked. "You pulled me in. I never wanted to be involved. This," he said, even closer now, standing over her. "It's your mess."

"Well, that's not how I see it," Culla replied, sounding calmer.

She doubted her gun was still in the holster. It would be the first thing Culla had taken. And they were close. Too close for her to run and stand any chance of getting away.

"It's you she came looking for. She's in your house," Culla continued. "They're all here, Les, in your house. If you back out now, it will look really bad for you. No one's going to believe *I* was involved. It doesn't matter that we're step-brothers. I'm a cop and cops protect cops."

"You bastard," West hissed.

"Don't be like that," Culla said. "We can make this right. She's been drinking, there are drugs in her system. All we have to do is get her in her car." His tone was insistent and confident at the same time.

She could tell by the back and forth *and* by Lester's exasperation that they'd been here before. *They're all here.* He was talking about the missing women. Connections were forming, and she could see the details coming together.

The newspaper clipping and the book Jane hid it in. The cover picture of a blonde man standing over a woman on the beach. She even wrote the word dunes on the clipping. It was Culla. He was the man Jane saw kill Adella.

"This is the last time," Culla said. "I swear."

The more she listened to them argue, the clearer her predicament became. She'd spent the last few years terrified of being back in this exact situation; helpless and hurt. Listening to Culla's plan, Veronika felt as though time had reversed itself and she was back in the most horrifying moment of her life. But this time, something was different.

This time, her thoughts were clearer and apart from a stiff shoulder and a lacerated arm, she was herself. With adrenaline pumping through her veins, she was prepared to fight. Culla might be able to manipulate Lester, but she could smell deceit, as thick and cloying as smoke in the air. Something was about to happen and she hoped it would give her the chance she needed.

"Look at this," Culla said.

He was moving away. She took a risk and opened her eyes. The two men were going into the back room. She waited, made herself count to three – slowly.

When she was alone, Veronika raised herself up, gritting her teeth as her left shoulder protested. She rolled it, first back and then forward. The seconds passed as slowly as a sleepless night. Each beat could mean the men's return. When the joint was moving freely, she grabbed the bottle of bleach.

From the back room, their voices carried.

"Go look outside, find her car and bring it up to the garage, but don't turn on the headlights," Culla instructed.

"Do you think I'm stupid?" Lester growled. "The minute I leave you alone with her you'll–"

A shot rang out.

She sprang to her feet. The room swam, and she caught the edge of the table for balance. She snatched her jacket off the table and searched the pockets, but her phone was gone. Brushing the hair out of her eyes, she realised her hand was sticky with blood. She didn't know who'd done the shooting, but one of them was armed.

With no time to waste, she slipped out of the kitchen and back into the sitting room. As she dashed for the front door, the kitchen door banged against the wall, telling her he was coming.

"Pope?" Culla called. "I'm not going to hurt you. I just want to talk."

Culla was looking for her and the gunshot told her that whatever co-dependent crimes the two men committed together, the relationship had soured. Culla had taken care of Lester and now it was her turn.

The front door was close and the safety chain was off, but she doubted she could get it open in time. Instead, she slapped her bloody hand on the wall next to the front door, then crept up the stairs.

She was almost at the top when Culla appeared in the hall. Veronika flattened herself against the wall. He didn't glance her way because his attention was on the handprint.

"Stupid bitch," he muttered and opened the door.

He stood for a moment; head cocked at an angle, looking out into the darkened street and the pouring rain. Veronika clamped her lips together and stayed pressed against the wall, willing him to go. One arm hung at his side with the gun pointed down. Another second passed before he stepped through the door and out of the house.

Still clutching the bottle of bleach, she bolted up the last few steps and around the corner. There wasn't much light filtering up from below. Enough to see there was nothing that she could use as a weapon and no sign of a landline. There were three doors, all of them closed, one on her left and two on the right. When she looked straight ahead, a figure moved, and she gasped. Not a figure, she realised, but her reflection in a mirror. Still breathing hard, she stuck her head around the corner and glanced downstairs.

The front door was open, but Culla was nowhere in sight. She let out a relieved breath, then noticed the smudge of blood on the wall halfway up the stairs. A second later, he appeared in the doorway and she pulled her head back.

Listening, she heard the front door slam. Then sounds of the safety chain rattling and then of him clomping through the house. Something smashed, and a door banged. Veronika made for the stairs, intent on getting out of the house, but stopped when Culla dashed back towards the front door. Hopefully, he would decide she *had* left the house and go looking for her. Her only plan was to wait a few seconds and follow him out. Get to a neighbour's house and use their phone to call for backup.

“I know you’re in here, Pope,” he said in an almost conversational tone. “Good trick with the handprint. Tricky thinking, that’s why they made you an inspector.” He laughed, the sound echoing up the stairs. “Blood on the wall. Is that another trick?”

She heard him climbing the stairs. With nowhere else to go, she opened the door on the left and slipped into the lightless room.

Chapter Thirty-seven

Showered and changed into a T-shirt and jeans – the jeans were on the snug side and the parmy and chips wouldn't help matters – Madge ordered a drink. It had been a hell of a day and she decided she'd worry about calories in the morning. When the beer arrived, she took it and headed for a booth at the far end of the bar. As she walked, a few people called out greetings, to which she nodded and raised a hand. Friday night, by six o'clock, the place would be heaving. By ten, things would go from merry to rowdy, at which time, she intended to be at home with her feet up.

Thinking of feet made her all too aware of how much hers were aching. She pulled out her phone and slapped it on the table, set her drink down, and slid into the booth. With the station in the capable hands of Shirly on the desk and dispatch, Colin could survive until closing time. With that in place, Madge had four hours until she was unofficially on call and incoming calls would be rerouted to her mobile. Not long, but enough time to enjoy one beer and a decent meal.

If the rain held, it would keep people off the streets. Not that much went down in Seabreak after dark. Not much that couldn't wait until morning. As badly as she wanted to switch off, Madge went over her to-do list for the following morning. Ashley Simcock was on her mind. With Jim out of action, the Simcock case would need to be handed to another detective. That would be Pope's call. The next move would be a warrant to search Ashley's bank records, but again, that would be on Pope. Part of the reason Madge had asked the detective inspector to dinner was to talk about the case. She also liked the woman and suspected under her stoic appearance, she might even be a laugh.

Madge checked her watch. It was getting late. If Pope didn't show in the next ten minutes, Madge intended to order without her. Strange, though, the inspector struck her as an efficient woman, not one to disappear without a text at least.

Pope said she had a couple of stops to make: Edward Wilson and Lester West. The calls could have gone long, Madge thought. Or was it something more serious? Pope was a capable woman, but after what Madge had witnessed that morning, she was all too aware of how quickly things could go sideways.

Beer untouched, Madge was evaluating the likelihood of West or Wilson being dangerous. Pope was only ten minutes late, but Madge had a bad feeling.

"Shit," she said to herself, a second later when her phone rang.

"Sergeant Nuse, this is DC Brian Costa of the Special Crime Squad."

Nuse listened as Detective Costa explained he was trying to locate DI Pope. She told him what she knew, and that Pope was ten minutes late for dinner.

"How likely is it?" Nuse asked, already pushing her drink aside and edging out of the booth. "That the DI would be late and not text?"

Costa didn't hesitate. "Highly unlikely."

* * *

By the time Madge jogged through the rain back to her car, her clothes were plastered to her body and her hair was hanging over her eyes. Not wanting to waste time returning to the station, she rubbed her hands dry on the passenger seat and called Shirly. It took the dispatcher a few minutes to find Lester West's address.

"Send Colin to Edward Wilson's house," Madge said. "Tell him to look out for the inspector's car and, Shirl, he needs to get inside that house." She paused for a second. "But tell him not to do anything stupid."

Her badge was in her pocket, but her gun was in the safe at the station. Hopefully, the badge would be enough.

The streets were slick and the bitumen shiny under the incessant rain. Madge stuck to the speed limit, drumming her fingers on the steering wheel in frustration. She had lived in Seabreak for eighteen months, but in the dark, on roads she'd never travelled, every turn looked the same.

Bushnell Road, a clumsy S-bend of a street, swooped west, skirting the beach at one point and then coming around to a sparse scattering of houses. Leaning forward with the wipers slapping rain off the windshield, Madge searched not for the house number but the iron fence. With the street lights in this area widely spaced, visibility was at a minimum. Her only hope was going from house to house – slowly. A few minutes of trawling along at walking speed and almost like an apparition, number eighty-one came in view.

Madge parked across the road and turned off the engine. Pope's car was nowhere in sight, but that meant little. There were plenty of side streets; the DI could have parked anywhere.

The lights were on in Lester's house, upstairs and ground floor. Before getting out of the car, she put in a call to Colin.

"Anything?" she asked when the constable answered.

"Nothing," he replied. "No car. Edward Wilson said she'd been there but left an hour ago. He let me inside to have a look around. Nothing."

"Okay," Nuse replied. "I'm at West's house." She gave him the address. "Get here as quick as you can."

A second later, she popped the boot and grabbed a long-barrelled metal torch from the back of the car. Despite the warm air, the rain was icy, and she cursed herself for not carrying a spare poncho. Braving the downpour, she dashed across the road, barely reaching the gate, when a shot rang out from the second storey. With the blast ringing in her ears, Madge ran for the front door.

Chapter Thirty-eight

Veronika closed the bedroom door as silently as possible. She could hear Culla on the landing. His feet squelched as he walked. All she could think of was what he'd said to Lester. *They're all here.* The words kept running over and over in her mind. All those missing women. Women for whom they'd searched so long and hard. Not just Veronika and her team, but the people before them – the police, their friends, the families.

A light shone under the door as he turned the landing light on. She heard a door open across the way. Unscrewing the cap on the bottle of bleach, she shuffled to the side of the door.

"I know you're up here." He sounded farther away, in one of the other rooms.

Her only hope against the gun was surprise. His search continued, and she heard cupboards opening and the scrape of furniture. She had one move. There could be no hesitating. Squelching feet. Her heart was beating in her throat when the knob rattled and the door opened.

His arm appeared, the left. He would be holding the gun in his right. She grabbed the arm and stepped out from the side of the door. Not expecting a front-on assault, he opened his mouth in surprise. In the same instant, Veronika jerked the bottle towards his face, tossing bleach into his eyes and mouth.

"What?" He sounded more startled than hurt.

Almost instantly, the surprise turned into pain and he was shrieking and coughing. He reached for his eyes with his free hand but she held on to his arm. He tried to raise the gun, so she pushed forward, throwing him off balance. They stumbled like clumsy dance partners with Culla's wet shoes slipping as he tried to stand his ground. Veronika bent her knees and used her shoulder, shoving him in the chest. Grunting with the effort and pain as something in the joint popped, she brought him to the head of the stairs.

Blind, Culla stumbled back, cursing and pawing at his face while trying to point the gun in her direction. His aim was off, so when he fired, the bullet flew by her face. The sound of the blast roared in her right ear like a sonic boom. He was bringing the gun around, ready to fire blind when she stepped back, raised her knee and kicked him in the chest.

He almost caught himself. Unable to see and grasping at air, his free hand landed on the banister and he took hold. If not for puddles on the stairs left by his wet shoes, he would have righted himself. His left foot slid out from under him. He went down. Falling backwards, arms pinwheeling, Culla hit the stairs. He cried out, a desperate yowl of pain and fear. He tried to grab for the baluster, but his body weight and momentum carried him.

Amidst the chaos, Veronika ducked low, knowing he still had the gun. She heard a voice, or at least thought someone called her name.

The fall took less than three seconds. Culla came to rest at the foot of the stairs. Left arm bunched in an unnatural heap against the baluster.

"You bitch," he howled. "You broke my fucking back."

Someone pounded on the front door. The safety chain rattled.

He still had the gun in his right hand. Culla struggled to raise the weapon. "Where are you?" He sounded crazed with anger and pain.

Veronika ducked lower and to her right. Behind Culla, the safety chain broke and a chunk of the door frame bounced onto the floorboards. Madge Nuse charged into the house. If Veronika hadn't seen it with her own eyes, she would never imagine the woman could move with such speed and accuracy.

Madge saw the gun and whacked Culla's arm with the barrel of what looked like a torch. Culla screamed. A full-bodied cry that reminded Veronika of a tortured animal. He dropped the gun to the floor and Madge kicked it away.

"You okay?" Madge asked, looking up at where Veronika now stood, cradling her arm.

"You broke my arm," Culla shrieked.

"Shut up," Madge snapped, her attention still on Veronika.

"I'm okay," Veronika replied, making her way down the stairs.

In the distance, a siren wailed.

Chapter Thirty-nine

They found Lester West. Critically injured but alive, he was transported, first by ambulance and then by helicopter, to Perth for emergency surgery. In the same back room, Veronika, Madge and Colin also discovered the body of a young woman wrapped in a plastic tarp.

"Ashley Simcock," Madge said, laying the flap of plastic back over the woman's face with a touch so gentle it belied the power she'd displayed only minutes earlier when she kicked the door in.

Culla, still conscious and claiming Veronika attacked him in his brother's home, was taken to the Seabreak Infirmary and treated for his injuries, then transferred by ambulance to Royal Perth Hospital. Before they loaded him into the ambulance with the green whistle clamped between his lips, Veronika placed him under arrest for assault and attempted murder.

"You're insane," Culla said dreamily as the Penthrox-filled inhaler slipped out of his mouth. "It wasn't me, it was my brother." His eyes were almost swollen shut from the effects of the bleach, giving his face the look of a depraved bullfrog.

The rain had stopped, but the street was still shiny under the moonlight. Veronika, not wanting to look at Culla for a moment more than was necessary, turned her back on the man and left Colin to accompany Culla to the hospital. She gladly accepted Madge's offer of a lift to the infirmary, but insisted they delay and wait with Ashley Simcock's body until the forensic team from Joondalup arrived.

"Thank you," Veronika said, once they were on their way to the hospital, "for coming in like that and, you know..."

"Breaking that asshole's arm?" Madge replied. "You looked like you had the situation under control. I just applied a little pressure in the right place."

Despite everything she'd been through, Veronika couldn't help laughing. "When you kicked that door in and hit him with the torch, I don't think I've ever seen anything like that."

Madge laughed too. It was a full-bodied, hearty sound. "You liked that? I call it my rock 'em, sock 'em move. Or, that's what I'm calling it from now on."

It was dark, the humour they found in such a deadly situation. But the laughter was healing, and it made the horrors of the experience feel a little less powerful. They both knew there was more horror to come. For them, but mostly for the victims' families. Laughter helped stave off the burden of delivering that horror.

* * *

Veronika was lying on a trolly, groggy from the pain meds they had given her while they reset her shoulder and flushed out the wound on her elbow. She wasn't in a room but in a curtained area in the treatment bay. It seemed the Special Crime Squad had maxed out the capabilities of the Seabreak Infirmary. But that was okay. The ticking in her brain had slowed, and she was feeling no pain – no physical pain. She would need a skin graft on her arm, the doctor said, but it could wait, for the time being anyway.

"I heard you had quite a night," Jim said, pulling open the curtain.

He was dressed in a hospital gown, with his bare legs sticking out from underneath the floaty fabric. Wearing socks and paper slippers, it struck her that there was something hilarious about his appearance. She wanted to laugh, but her face felt too heavy.

"It's not as bad as it looks," she replied, looking down at the sling and bandages. "You should see the other guy." This time she did laugh, but it was a sleepy sound.

"I did," Jim replied. "He's here too. They're transporting him to Perth in the morning. Stacey's driving to pick us up tomorrow. I can't say I won't be glad to leave this town."

"Not my idea of a holiday spot," she replied, struggling to keep her eyes open.

"Culla took my phone. I'm supposed to organise lunch for Tony." She was having trouble getting the words out. "I need to call and let them know."

"I'll do it," Jim said.

"Don't scare my mother." Veronika's voice was thick with sleep.

"I won't. Now, I'll let you get some sleep." Before he turned to leave, Jim stopped. "You got him, Vee."

The last part was lost on her because she was already asleep.

Chapter Forty

Two weeks after Robert Culla's arrest, the story of the killer cop was making headlines, not just in Australia, but in many corners of the world. Culla – with a broken collarbone, two broken ribs, a fractured ulna and radius, as well as tissue damage to his right eye – was remanded in custody and then transferred to the prison infirmary. Ironically, Culla alleged the two officers who apprehended him had used excessive force. In light of Veronika's injuries and Madge Nuse's corroborating statement, a formal inquiry was closed after three days.

On their way to Casuarina Prison Infirmary to formally read Culla the list of upgraded charges, Brian and Veronika listened to the latest news report on the radio.

> *In what some are calling the Killer Cop House, police are still excavating the site in Seabreak, where it is believed that multiple grisly murders occurred. Crimes that stretch back over twenty years. Police have formally identified the body of twenty-eight-year-old Ashley Simcock, who went missing only days before former police sergeant Robert Culla was arrested.*
>
> *In a shocking development on the search for missing newlywed, Jane Wilson, police have revealed that four*

more bodies have been recovered. It's believed that Jane Wilson is among the victims but police have yet to confirm their identities.

"Do you think we'll get anything out of him?" Brian asked, turning the radio off.

"More denials," Veronika answered. "But let's see how he reacts to the latest developments."

* * *

Robert Culla, propped up on pillows with one eye patched, looked shrunken. Even his blonde hair appeared thinner and stringy with grease. With a prison guard standing at the door, Veronika and Brian pulled plastic chairs up to the bed and made themselves comfortable.

"How's the arm, Inspector?" Culla asked with a glint of sarcasm in his eye.

"Better than ever," Veronika replied. "You know why we're here?"

Culla's one visible eye shone as he looked from her to Brian and back again. She didn't expect him to talk. In fact, what she really wanted was for him to listen. To listen and understand that it was over for him. She wanted to see the realisation dawn on his face and take that with her when she spoke to the victims' families.

"Before I read the charges, I'd like to tell you my version of events," she said, giving him a tight smile. "I think you might be surprised."

When he didn't respond, Veronika began. "In 2000, as a constable stationed at Seabreak Police Station, you met Jane Wilson, née Campion, when her mother called in a noise complaint. You only saw her for a moment, but then, the next night when you murdered Adella Reece in the sand dunes, you saw Jane again. She saw you and you saw her. But she got away before you could stop her. What could you do? Jane was a child on holiday with her parents. It's not like you could burst into her parents' house and snatch her."

Veronika spread her arms wide. "You must have thought you'd got lucky when Jane didn't come forward with what she saw. You literally got away with murder, but that wasn't enough for you, was it, Bob?" Veronika didn't wait for him to answer. "After murdering Adella, you had a taste for it. In 2007, you abducted and murdered Candice Burns, a young woman from Ledge Point. I'm guessing that you were obsessed with Adella but Candice was just for thrills. You saw her when she was arrested or at the petrol station and you just couldn't resist.

"Fifteen years after murdering Adella, Jane came back to town. This is where the story gets foggy," Veronika said. "But we will circle back in a minute. You couldn't let her live, not once she saw you, and she did see you, didn't she?"

Veronika waited, but Culla turned his head so he was looking straight ahead, eye fixed on the wall.

"Jane Wilson was last seen on the back steps of Richard and Edward Wilson's house. You watched the house, snuck around the back and murdered Jane. By then, your compulsion to kill was growing. You liked it. *And* you couldn't stop."

She turned to Brian. "What do you think?"

"Mummy issues?" Brian offered.

"Shut up!" Culla screamed. "You shut your mouth or I'll–"

Brian sat forward in his chair, leaning closer to Culla. "I think I hit a nerve."

"I don't have to listen to this shit," Culla hissed, but pulled back into his pillows. "Not from an upstart like you."

"Settle down," the guard near the door, a large stocky man with a thick Scottish accent, ordered Culla.

"You were the first officer to interview Richard after his wife went missing," Veronika said, ignoring Culla's outburst. "When you handed the case over to Detective Bender, you told him Richard Wilson was as guilty as sin.

You planted a seed in Bender's mind and suddenly, Richard was the prime suspect. And you got away with murder *again*.

"Four years ago, you attacked Veeta Seckov, but she fought you off. Losing your touch?" Veronika paused. "You were getting old, Bob, but you weren't ready to stop. Three years ago, you murdered Lacy Walmer. Seventeen years old, just a kid. So that makes you a child killer."

Veronika turned to Brian. "I've heard child killers have a rough time inside."

"A one-eyed child killer *and* an ex-cop." Brian whistled. "They call that dog meat."

"How am I doing so far, Bob?" Veronika asked, turning back to the man in the bed.

"Why don't you just charge me and get out," Culla snapped.

"What I couldn't work out was how you knew Jane Wilson was back in Seabreak," Veronika continued, as though Culla hadn't spoken. "Richard said they didn't see anyone, but then it clicked. They stopped at the petrol station and Jane waited outside. In the case file, Bender noted talking to the girl that worked at the petrol station, Linda. She confirmed that Richard Wilson had stopped there the day before Jane went missing. He bought two drinks. Linda never saw Jane, but you did.

"You saw her, didn't you? You were there to see your stepbrother and spotted a face from your past. Jane, all grown up. You knew Richard Wilson and his brother. You knew where they lived." Veronika watched Culla's face, but saw only anger.

"But why kill Jason Reece? What did he know?" she asked, not expecting an answer. "That part puzzled me."

"I had nothing to do with any of it," Culla said. "I'm going to sue you, Pope, and the department. I'm going to ruin you."

Veronika gave him another polite smile. "Your stepbrother is doing well by the way. A punctured lung. Nasty, but he'll make a good recovery."

Culla's face changed, and for the first time, she saw fear.

"He's been very helpful. Nothing like a bullet in the lung to get you talking, if you know what I mean. Your stepbrother is being very cooperative. In fact, he's agreed to give testimony in return for a reduction in the charges against him. *He* won't die in prison."

She waited a few seconds before continuing, "Lester said you killed Jason Reece because if we spoke to him, he would have mentioned that the four of you were once good friends; you, Lester, Adella and Jason. Friends until Adella couldn't stand the sight of you. Lester said you were afraid that once your name was in the mix, I'd start digging."

"He's lying," Culla spat. "Lester killed those women, not me. His word against mine."

"Not quite," Veronika said. "I heard you tell Lester pretty much the same thing the night you tried to kill me. I heard you tell him no one would believe him. So, it's my word as well as his," she gave him a beat to absorb what she was saying. "Lester said he never touched the bodies, but you did. *You* touched them plenty. I guess we'll see what the DNA tests come back with.

"And then there's the shoe print from the site where we found Ashley Simcock's earring. Size ten and a perfect match with the tread on the shoes you were wearing the night you were arrested. Your shoes, not Lester's. It's a small piece of the puzzle, but every little bit helps," she added.

He opened his mouth to say something, then snapped it shut. Whatever bluster he had when the meeting began was slipping away under the weight of evidence against him. Veronika wondered if Culla's plan had always been to use his stepbrother as the fall guy if things went wrong.

And the last step in Culla's plan was to kill Lester so he couldn't defend himself against the allegations.

According to Lester, he'd only ever covered up for Culla and had no actual involvement in the crimes. If that was true, and Veronika didn't believe it was that simple, it meant Lester had allowed his stepbrother to use his house as a base while he murdered multiple women. Whatever the arrangement, Lester would spend at least twelve years in prison. Robert Culla would die behind bars. Charging him and putting him away for his crimes should have been enough, but Veronika wanted to leave him with as little mercy as he'd shown his victims.

"You know, Bob," she said in a more conversational tone. "The first time I met you, I thought, now there's a man who knows how to duck and weave. And I was right because you've managed to go through life, work, maybe even social situations without ever being found out.

"You were always playing a part. But underneath, there's nothing human about you. That part is missing," she continued, while Culla watched her with growing agitation. "Do you feel it, Bob? Do you feel like an outsider? A monster wearing human skin?"

"I don't have to listen to this," he said through clenched teeth. "Get out."

"I can't do that, Bob. Not until I'm finished with you," she replied.

Veronika straightened herself in her chair. "Robert Culla," she began, "I'm charging you with the wilful murder of Adella Reece, Candice Burns, Jane Wilson and Ashley Simcock, attempted murder of a police officer, assault on a public officer and assault on Veeta Seckov. We'll be adding a fifth and sixth count of wilful murder to those charges when we formally identify the body believed to be that of Lacy Walmer and when the autopsy results on Jason Reece are handed down."

She continued, explaining Culla's rights while the man glowered at her from the bed.

When they left the prison and returned to the car, Brian paused with the driver's door open. "What about what Lester said about Culla pushing his mother down the stairs when they were kids?"

"We could give it a fly, include it in the charges, but there's no proof." Veronika stared back at the prison. "In the end, it would only muddy the waters. And, with a man like Culla, we'll never know the whole story."

Veronika took a deep breath. Even the air around the prison smelled heavy with industrial cleaner and boiled food. This would be the air Robert Culla breathed for the rest of his life. Was it enough after the things he'd done? The misery he'd caused? Probably not, but it was all they had.

Brian's phone buzzed. "Give me a second," he said and stepped away from the car.

As she opened the car door, her elbow twinged. The skin graft went well and her arm was healing, but it would still be another couple of weeks until she could drive herself.

"Philip Olsen was able to confirm Lacy Walmer's identity," Brian said, climbing behind the wheel. "The pink tattoo and a dolphin ring. He said he didn't want to be involved, but when I told him we thought we'd found her, he stepped up." Brian let out a tired breath. "Looks like he's the only one who was willing to come through for her. No one in that girl's life missed her enough to file a missing person's report. Lacy's father lives in Katanning. He said he wasn't interested when the coroner's office called him."

He appeared lost in thought for a moment. "Philip is paying for the funeral, too. I guess he feels he could have done more to help her."

"She's in safe hands now, at least," Veronika replied.

"I keep thinking about Dr Sharm," Brian said. "He's not the same as Culla, but the man is a predator nonetheless."

"So, what now?" she asked, knowing the answer.

"I've drafted a letter to The Psychology Board of Australia informing them of Sharm's conduct. I'm sending it off tonight," Brian replied. "If he'd listened, paid attention to what Jane was trying to tell him, maybe she'd still be alive. But he used her fragility for his own purposes. In many ways, he's no better than Culla."

Brian was right, but Jane had been surrounded by people who didn't pay enough attention. People who couldn't or wouldn't hear what she was trying to tell them. Her parents, her husband; there was plenty of blame to go around. They'd paid the ultimate price and would continue to do so for the rest of their lives. Sharm was another matter. He had an ethical and professional responsibility to his patient. He failed Jane and exploited his position of power when he entered into a sexual relationship with her.

"Best case," Veronika said, "Sharm loses his licence to practise psychology and he'll never be able to do the same thing to another woman."

When Brian didn't answer, she continued. "We'll never stop all of them, but Culla, West and Sharm are a good start. It has to be enough or you'll drive yourself crazy."

"I put that CD back in evidence," Brian replied.

"Good. Now come on," Veronika said, "we've got another stop to make."

Chapter Forty-one

"Have you told her parents?" Richard asked.

This was Veronica's last stop for the day. A day which began with confirming what Jane Wilson's mother and father had known for seven years. They'd known it in their hearts even if they dared not speak it aloud. Their daughter was dead, buried under a thin layer of concrete in the back room of Lester West's house. All their darkest fears were finally and irrevocably confirmed.

The utter finality of Veronika's words brought neither relief nor comfort. They fell like blows, battering the elderly couple before Veronika's eyes. At least in grief, they turned to each other. Stephen holding Marian as she wept. Who, she thought, would Richard turn to?

"Yes," she replied. "I visited them this morning."

Richard nodded. "Can I offer you tea?"

They drank tea together. This time, Richard sat beside her and they both faced the river. Another sunny day in paradise.

"Jane wanted to live by the river," he said. "That's why I bought this place. We were supposed to have a family. All *I* have is an empty apartment, but she was never really mine. Not for long anyway."

"You're still Jane's next of kin," Veronika said. "When her body is released, you can bury her. You can give her that."

"No," Richard replied. "That right belongs to her parents. I won't take that from them."

It was a kind gesture. More than she had expected from such a controlled man, especially after the Campions had vilified him as a murderer. But maybe she'd misjudged him. She almost told him so. Almost tried to offer comfort by telling him it was over at last. But in truth, it would never be over for Richard or Jane's parents. When cases like Jane's were solved, there were no real victors, only fresh pain.

"I'm sorry," Richard said, surprising her. "For the last time you were here. I behaved badly. I have no excuse."

"No need for apologies," she replied. "But there is one thing I need to know."

Richard faced her, waiting. That guarded look, the one she'd seen the first time she met him, had long vanished.

"Your brother said you once smoothed things over with Culla after he picked Edward up and threatened to go to your father. How did you do that?" she asked.

It was a small thing. Not even a detail that mattered to the case, but it had puzzled her.

"I offered him two hundred dollars to drop the matter," he said with flat honesty. "He accepted."

When Richard walked her to the door, he stopped her before she left. "They haven't said on the news, but Adella?"

It always came back to Adella. From the moment she read her file and looked at her photo, this end was inevitable. The moment she looked into the woman's dark troubled eyes, Veronika knew. Not the details. How could she have possibly envisioned the length and breadth of the case? What she knew was that Adella was the key to Jane's disappearance.

"Yes," she replied. "She was there with Jane."

These were the worst days. Worse than the aftermath of a life and death battle, worse than the bodies and the smell. Carrying the heartbreak from house to house was the heaviest of cargos.

Madge had shouldered some of the burden, agreeing to take the news to Ashley Simcock's mother and later to Candice Burns's parents.

Veronika had planned on visiting Elizabeth Crozier in the morning, but decided the woman had waited long enough. So, there would be one more stop on Veronika's march of sadness. One more stop before she could go home to her family and the warmth of knowing her loved ones were safe.

The End

If you enjoyed this book, please let others know by leaving a quick review on Amazon. Also, if you spot anything untoward in the paperback, get in touch. We strive for the best quality and appreciate reader feedback.

editor@thebookfolks.com

www.thebookfolks.com

Also by Anna Willett

In this series:

THE WOMAN BEHIND HER
THE FAMILY MAN

The Lucy Hush series:

SMALL TOWN NIGHTMARE
COLD VALLEY NIGHTMARE
SAVAGE BAY NIGHTMARE

Thrillers and horror:

BACKWOODS RIPPER
RETRIBUTION RIDGE
UNWELCOME GUESTS
FORGOTTEN CRIMES
CRUELTY'S DAUGHTER
VENGEANCE BLIND
PEST
BEST
DEAR NEIGHBOUR
LOST TO THE LAKE

THE WOMAN BEHIND HER (Book 1)

When Jackie Winter inherits her aunt's house, she makes a chilling discovery. Worse, she feels that she is being watched. When someone is murdered nearby, she finds herself in the frame. Can she join up the dots and prove her innocence?

THE FAMILY MAN (Book 2)

During a home renovation, terrifying video footage of torture is discovered. With little to go on save a blurry image of one victim's face, Senior Sergeant Veronika Pope is tasked with tracking down an evil, methodical killer.

Other titles of interest

PENURY by Pete Brassett

James Munro is busy minding other people's business out of town when he stumbles upon an unfortunate DI Greg Byrne who is out of his depth dealing with a garish murder. Offering a helping hand, Munro soon realizes there are connections with a case closer to home. Will it be his new star pupil or his old protégé DI Charlie West who'll bring home the bacon?

A VIEW TO MURDER by Robert McNeill

When a student is found dead within the crags in Edinburgh's Holyrood Park, DI Jack Knox must make sense of her friends' conflicting stories about the events that led up to her death. But his boss risks putting a spanner in the works when Knox is asked to act as a go-between in a deadly drugs sting.

THE
BOOK
FOLKS

Made in the USA
Middletown, DE
02 February 2023